ALD

Girlfriends

"Hi," said Keri. "Want to come to a party?"

"Ooh, yes, please!" I said. I love parties.

"I've already asked Lily," said Keri. "She's going to come."

"What about Frizz?" I said. Me and Frizz, Lily and Keri, we're the Gang of Four. We're all at separate schools, now, but we'd sworn an oath, back last summer when we were still at Juniors, that come what may, through thick and thin, we would stick together.

Keri said, "What d'ya mean, what about Frizz?"

"Aren't you going to ask her?"

"Of course I'm going to ask her!" Keri sounded indignant. "What do you think? I wouldn't ask you and Lily without asking Frizz! Why would I ask you and not her?"

I hadn't really thought she would try leaving Frizz out. I mean we always did things together: it was part of our oath that we had sworn...but once or twice, just lately, Keri had seemed a bit impatient with poor old Frizz... Just because Frizz wasn't growing up quite as fast as the rest of us!

Also by Jean Ure
in the Girlfriends series

Pink Knickers Aren't Cool!
Girls Stick Together!
Boys Are OK!

Orchard Black Apples

Get a Life
Just 16
Love is for Ever

ORCHARD BOOKS
338 Euston Road, London NW1 3BH
Orchard Books Australia
Hachette Children's Books
Level 17/207 Kent Street, Sydney, NSW 2000

ISBN 978 1 84616 962 5

First published in 2002 by Orchard Books
This edition published in 2008
A paperback original

Text © Jean Ure 2002
The right of Jean Ure to be identified as the author of
this work has been asserted by her in accordance with the
Copyright, Designs and Patents Act, 1988.

A CIP catalogue record for this book is available from the British Library.

1 3 5 7 9 10 8 6 4 2
Printed in Great Britain

Orchard Books is a division of Hachette Children's Books,
an Hachette Livre UK company

www.orchardbooks.co.uk

Girls Are Groovy!

JEAN URE

ORCHARD BOOKS

Chapter 1

I was upstairs in my bedroom, rolling about with Bundle (he's my dog) when Mum called up to me. "Pollee! Keri's on the phone!"

I said, "Keri?" Keri doesn't ring me all that often. It's usually me and Frizz that ring each other.

I charged downstairs and snatched up the phone. "Keri?" I said. "Hi!"

"Hi," said Keri. "Want to come to a party?"

"Ooh, yes, please!" I said. I love parties. "Is it a New Year's one?"

"Yes. It's a pool party. To celebrate our pool."

I knew about Keri's pool. Well, her mum and dad's pool, really. The reason I knew was that my dad was the one who had put it in! It's what he does, he puts pools in for people. But he doesn't very often put them *inside* their houses! They're mostly outside in the garden and would probably be fre-e-e-ezing on New Year's Eve. But Keri's mum and dad are simply stupendously rich, and this is the sort of thing that you can do when you are rich...have heated pools inside your house! If ever I am rich that is what I am going to do. And I am going to swim in it morning and night and three times on a Sunday. I can think of nothing more blissful!

"We've got a sauna, as well," said Keri. "And a jacuzzi."

"Is that one of those things you whizz round in?" I said.

"Yes, but it's not working properly yet. When it is you can all come over and we'll whizz round like crazy! New Year's is just for the pool. Your mum and dad are invited, too, natch! Your dad's here right now. Mum's just asked him."

"Did he say yes?" I said. You never know, with Dad. Sometimes Mum complains he's a bit of a stay-at-home. But Keri said he'd promised he and Mum would go, so that was all right. Hooray! What a fab place to hold a party...in a pool!

"I've already asked Lily," said Keri. "She's going to come."

"What about Frizz?" I said. Me and Frizz, Lily and Keri, we're the Gang of Four. We're all at separate schools, now, but we'd sworn an oath, back last summer when we were still at Juniors, that come what may, through thick and through thin, we would stick together.

Keri said, "What d'you mean, what about Frizz?"

"Aren't you going to ask her?"

"Of course I'm going to ask her!" Keri sounded indignant. "What do you think? I wouldn't ask you and Lily without asking Frizz! Why would I ask you and not her?"

"I don't know," I said.

"Well, I wouldn't! You've got some nerve!"

"Sorry," I said. "Sorry!"

"So I should think," grumbled Keri.

I hadn't really thought she would try leaving Frizz out. I mean we just always did things together: it was part of our oath that we had sworn. But Lily is Keri's best friend, so she was bound to have asked her; and my dad was the one who had put the pool in, so she was bound to have asked me; but once or twice, just lately, Keri had seemed a bit impatient with poor old Frizz. Like pulling faces at things she said, or making these clicking noises with her tongue when Frizz did something she thought was stupid. Just because Frizz wasn't growing up quite as fast as the rest of us! Whereas Keri has always been so cool it is unbelievable. And even cooler now she was at her posh boarding school.

"I was going to ring her after I'd rung you," said Keri. "She could come with you and your mum and dad, right?"

"Right." I nodded. Frizz would like that! So would I. Maybe, if Mum and Dad were going to be there, we could even stay right through till midnight and sing *Auld Lang Syne*.

"But, look," said Keri, "do tell her to wear something a bit funky!"

"Me?" I said. "Why me?" Keri is our style queen!

"'Cos you'll know what to say to her," said Keri. "I don't want to go and upset her. I just don't want her turning up looking like Humpty Dumpty in a bin bag!"

I giggled at that; and then stopped myself. I don't like to be disloyal to Frizz.

"It's for her own sake," said Keri. "If she doesn't

learn to dress properly she'll never get *anywhere*."

I suppose this is right, though it is very easy when you look like Keri – tall and slim with long red hair that's all foamy and springy. Also when your mum and dad have stacks of money, which Frizz's mum and dad do not. Nor do mine, and neither am I tall and slim, but rather round and short, with a roundish face and hair of no particular colour. Plus I wear glasses, which I hate! But in spite of this I do try to be just a *little* bit cool.

As soon as I said goodbye to Keri I rushed upstairs to my room, sat down at my workstation that I'd had for Christmas, opened my lovely new diary and solemnly made an entry for 31st December:

POOL PARTY AT KERI'S!

I underlined it three times and then highlighted it in yellow. Last term I'd got into a bit of a muddle with my (ahem!) social engagements. I'd kept double-booking and then flying into panics and having to ring people at the last minute saying that I couldn't do what I said I'd do on account of stupidly having arranged to go and do something else. My biggest New Year's resolution was: TO BE EFFICIENT. From now on, I was going to record every single thing in my diary!

Something else I wrote down was:

NB: HELP FRIZZ LOOK FUNKY!

If Frizz had been Chloë (who is my best friend at school) we would have been on the phone for simply hours discussing what we were going to wear to the party. But although Frizz is my best *home* friend, and in fact my very best friend of all time, clothes were not something we ever really talked about. I don't know whether it was because Frizz simply wasn't interested or because she just didn't have any.

On New Year's Eve I wore a cowgirl top – red, with a little purple cowgirl going "Yee Hah!" – and my silver stars jeans. Mum, as usual, wanted me to wear "something pretty". Mum just has *no idea* what's cool!

I went round to Frizz's early so that I could supervise her and decide what she should put on, only to discover that there was almost nothing in her wardrobe that could even be described as wearable, let alone funky!

Frizz kept hopefully dragging stuff out and going, "What about this? Couldn't I wear this?" And I would take one look and cringe, 'cos I knew that Keri would only roll her eyes and pull one of her faces. She would think it was something I had chosen. I didn't want Keri thinking that!

"What's the matter with these?" Frizz would say holding up a pair of truly horrible trousers made out of some kind of floppy material.

And I would go, "No-o-o! Frizz, you *can't*!"

And Frizz just wouldn't be able to see why not. She just couldn't see what was wrong with them. I tried my best not to get impatient 'cos getting impatient doesn't help, it just tends to fluster her. I said, "Look, I know it's stupid and it shouldn't really matter, but it's, like, a *pool* party, you know? A cool pool party! So we've all got to look a little bit funky."

I couldn't even have lent her anything of mine as we are totally different sizes. Frizz is loads taller than I am. And maybe not quite as *round*, though she is not slim like Keri. She doesn't really have what I would call a shape, though maybe she will grow into one. Mum says this is what usually happens.

In the end I managed to find a shirt that wasn't too bad – "It's one of my school ones!" wailed Frizz – and a pair of black trousers that were reasonably OK. Like at least no one was going to look at her and think, "Oh, that girl is so uncool!"

"What about my hair?" she said. "Keri will go mad if I don't do something with my hair! Can't you style it for me? The way she did?"

Keri does things with hair that are totally brilliant! She loops it and scoops it and twizzles it all about. I can't do that with mine. Mine is too short to be looped or scooped or twizzled. Frizz's can be, but I am not very inventive when it comes to hair. I looped a bit, and I twizzled a bit, and Frizz's face looked at me from the mirror, all eager and trusting, and I thought, "Help! This isn't working!" I then had a clever idea (they come to me, sometimes) and tried pulling it back into a big sausagey plait. Which worked! It worked really well!

"Is it OK?" Frizz studied herself, anxiously. "I don't want Keri being mad at me!"

I said, "She won't be mad at you. It looks fantastic!"

"Do you really think so?" said Frizz.

I said, "Yes, I do, and anyway who cares what Keri thinks?"

That is what I *said*, but I am such a hypocrite! 'Cos I did care what Keri thought. I had this feeling that I shouldn't, but I just couldn't seem to stop myself. It is so pathetic!

I'd gone to Frizz's on the bus. Mum and Dad came by later in the car, with Craig, to pick us up. Craig is my brother. He is nearly two years older than me and goes to a different school. Thank goodness. He is all right, I suppose. Most of the time. *Some* of the time. When he is not trying to embarrass me and calling me Poll Doll just to annoy. Frizz went bright red simply at the sight of him. Craig said, "Ho, 'tis Frizzle Frazzle and the Poll Doll!" He says things like this all the time. Totally futile. It's because he's a boy.

Boys – *yuck* is the way I feel.

There were several boys at the party. Keri assured us that *she* hadn't invited them. She said, "They belong to people." Meaning, people that her mum and dad had invited.

Keri might not have invited any boys, but she had invited a girl from her school. A girl called Jemima, who lived in the country and had a pony. We knew all about Jemima, 'cos Keri had told us…loads of times!

"I didn't know she was going to invite anyone else," whispered Frizz.

"No," I said. "Nor did I."

There wasn't any reason Keri shouldn't have invited Jemima if that's what she wanted to do, but I had this feeling she might have told us. I mean, we were the Gang of Four! It just didn't seem right.

I wondered how Lily felt about it, Lily being Keri's

oldest friend; but Lily didn't seem especially bothered. She was just eager to get in the pool. She kept dancing round going, "When can we swim, when can we swim?"

Keri's mum laughed and said, "Whenever you like!"

"No, you've got to wait for me!" shrieked Keri. "Bags I first in!"

It was odd, considering it was a pool party, but not a single one of the grown-ups went for a swim! Keri said they were probably too bothered about their hair.

"They've had it all done specially. Love the way you've done yours!" she added, to Frizz.

Frizz immediately turned bright scarlet with pleasure. "Polly did it," she mumbled.

"It's great! It suits you, you should always wear it like that. See, you can go in the water and it won't matter. But if you'd had it all washed and set and sprayed and—"

"My mum hasn't had it all washed and set and sprayed," I said. "She could go in."

"She could," said Keri, "but if it's not their hair, it's their figures...all saggy and baggy so they don't want people looking at them!"

I thought this was a bit unfair as some of the mums

– Keri's, for instance – were slim as could be. (Not mine, 'cos she's a short stumpy person like me!) And what about the dads? Who cared what they looked like? Grown-ups are so odd! They enjoy themselves in ways that I would consider totally boring. While we splashed around in the lovely warm water, they just stood around in little huddles, talking.

We could all swim, except for Frizz, who for some reason had just never learnt. Keri, who is absolutely mega sporty, can do the crawl and the backstroke and also dive. She kept leaping off the top board and slicing down into the water. She must have known that people were admiring her 'cos every time she did it there was a little burst of clapping.

Frizz giggled and said, "Keri's getting a figure… she's got *boobs*!"

I felt my face go bright scarlet. I didn't know which way to look! *Frizz*, talking about *boobs*! Boobs is one of those words, along with certain others such as – um – well! Bust, for instance. Bra, for instance. That always used to make me blush. (I don't do it now, of course. I am speaking about when I was ten years old.)

Frizz was still giggling. "She'll get top heavy if she carries on like that!"

Oh, dear! This was most embarrassing! I turned

away and stared fixedly across the pool to where Keri's pony friend, Jemima – wearing a really *snazzy* bikini – was making eyes at Craig. I can't imagine why she bothered, as he is not at all hunky, but all the other boys were like about nine or ten, which probably she thought was beneath her. She was obviously man-mad.

Lily was bobbing up and down like a cork, just nearby. She can't really swim properly, but she does this mad dog-paddle which whizzes her about all over the place, while I can only do a rather slow and boring breaststroke which whizzes me nowhere at all. I can just about manage one length of the baths. But at least I wouldn't drown! If I was in a boat and it sank, for example.

"Just going to go and do some swimming," I said to Frizz.

I felt a bit mean leaving her all by herself in the shallow end but I did want to show people that I wasn't absolutely useless. If I'd stayed with her they might have thought that I couldn't swim. Anyway, I kept going back to her, and Lily dog-paddled all round her in a big circle, so it wasn't like she was totally ignored.

After a while, Frizz clambered out and I went to

join her. We wrapped ourselves up in big stripy towels and sat together, by the edge of the pool, dibbling our toes in the water.

Frizz said, "You didn't have to get out just because of me."

"I didn't," I said. "I wanted to."

I could tell she didn't believe me, but in fact it was true. I had quite enjoyed doing my breaststroke, but I felt far happier just sitting in a huddle with Frizz. It felt right, somehow. Me and Frizz together. I just feel – well! – comfortable with her. I suppose it is because we have known each other for so long.

While we were sitting, wrapped in our towels, Lily sprang out of the pool and started dancing. Lily dances wherever she is! It's not that she shows off. It's just that this urge comes over her, and she can't resist. She'd do it even if she were by herself. She looked like a little green elf (her bathing cozzie was green) as she pranced up and down. Everybody stopped what they were doing and watched her, because people always watch Lily.

I heard someone behind us, saying, "What a fantastic little mover that girl is!" Then I heard Keri's mum, explaining how Lily went to this famous dance school and was training to be a dancer.

"It shows, doesn't it? You just feel compelled to watch her."

When Keri's mum said that, I got this little twingly sensation. I wasn't jealous; not exactly. But I couldn't help thinking how good it would make you feel if you could do something special that made people want to watch. I couldn't do anything special. I couldn't sing, I couldn't dance, I couldn't play a musical instrument. I couldn't dive, I couldn't skate, I couldn't ride horses. I was just totally and utterly nondescript. Just a *blob*.

On the other hand, I had been chosen to learn Latin! Starting from next term. I bet nobody at the pool party knew Latin! It was only the top French set that were allowed to do it. You had to be really good at languages. Me and Chloë had both been picked.

I wondered what people would say if I suddenly jumped up and shouted, *"I'm going to learn Latin!"* Probably they would think I was mad. But they might also think I was clever! I wouldn't do it, of course. I am one of those people, I am quite embarrassed to draw attention to myself. But it would be nice if someone just suddenly started talking about it and said (for instance), "I don't suppose there's anybody here that's going to learn Latin?" And then I could say that I was, and it wouldn't matter if I grew all hot and red, at least everyone would know, and I wouldn't be boasting.

Lily finished off her dance with a twiddly sort of twirl and a curtsey, and everyone clapped.

"Lily is so dainty," said Frizz. "I love to watch her when she dances!"

There wasn't even a *trace* of envy in Frizz's voice. I have never known Frizz to be envious. She is always the first to say generous things. She may not be the coolest of us, or the cleverest, or the prettiest, but I do think she is far and away the nicest!

We stayed at the party till the clock struck twelve, when we all joined hands and sang *Auld Lang Syne* and rushed about kissing and hugging. I kissed Frizz, and Frizz kissed me, then Lily and Keri came bundling over and we all kissed each other. Out of the corner of my eye I saw Jemima in a clinch with Craig (she was welcome!) and I just felt so glad that she wasn't trying to push her way in with the rest of us. She had been a right pain all evening, flashing about in her snazzy bikini and speaking in this really LOUD voice. She wasn't one of us! She didn't belong!

"Friends for ever!" cried Keri. "Happy New Year!"

And then Jemima couldn't resist it but had to come barrelling over going shriek, hoot, wah! and it all broke up. But by then I didn't mind so much because we'd had our moment. And on Saturday we were all meeting up again, like we did every Saturday; and by then, as I said to Frizz, *"She'll be gone!"*

We'd be just us, the Gang of Four. Which is how we like it!

Chapter 2

Ho! Well. Guess what? I was wrong! She hadn't gone – Jemima, I mean. Come Saturday she was still there, all loud and clangy, draped over the sofa in Keri's sitting room like she owned the place.

When we'd made our vow about staying together, we'd also made a vow that we would meet every weekend, just the four of us. We didn't always meet at Keri's place even though it was the biggest and the poshest. We took it in turns. One week my place, one week Frizzle's, one week Lily's. All our places are quite humble compared to Keri's. Me and Lily live in small houses on big estates, and Frizz lives over her mum and dad's shop, down town. Frizz's bedroom is tucked away in the attic, and really tiny, but we always have a good time there. We have fun!

We don't have any more fun at Keri's, simply because she has her own sitting room. And now an indoor pool! It was just coincidence that it was our turn for meeting at her place right after the party.

"We'll go and have a swim first," said Keri, "then we'll come back up here and have tea."

We always have to do what Keri says. Well, it seems to me we do. Even when we're not at her place. Lily is so easy, she never bothers to argue. She just goes along with whatever Keri decides. The only time Lily ever gets stubborn and digs her heels in is if it's something to do with her dancing. Then she can get really snakey! Nothing is allowed to come between Lily and her dancing. Frizz doesn't argue 'cos she's just naturally obedient; she is quite a meek sort of person. I am the only one who gets bolshy! That is what my dad calls it when I answer back or won't do what I'm told. He says, "Don't you get bolshy with me, Miss!"

Well, I felt bolshy today. 'Cos I suppose, secretly, I

was a bit miffed about Jemima still being there. Plus Keri was going through one of those phases when she was just so-o-o-o pleased with herself.

"Is that what we've all decided?" I said.

Everybody looked at me. The Jemima person looked at me as if I was completely batty.

"What do you mean?" said Keri. "*Is that what we've all decided?*"

"About going and having a swim. I mean...is that what you decided before me and Frizz got here?"

Keri said, "No. Why?"

"I just wondered," I said. It wasn't that I didn't want to have a swim; I just felt she should have consulted us.

Bolshy!

"Well, we can hardly eat first," said Keri. "We've only just had lunch."

"And anyway," (that was the Jemima person, all self-important), "you shouldn't go into the water right after eating."

I ignored this. Like, I mean, everybody *knows* about not going swimming on a full stomach. It gives you cramp. I'm not stupid!

"What's your problem?" said Keri.

There was a pause, while I thought what to say.

"I haven't brought my swimming costume," suddenly burst out Frizz.

"So go nude!" cried Lily. She giggled. "We could all go nude!"

"Skinny dipping!" shrieked Jemima.

Frizz looked startled. "I'm not going nude!"

"Nor am I." I glared in challenging fashion at Keri. I do feel that someone has to stand up to her. I mean, she would otherwise just get way too big for her boots. "I'm not going nude!"

It's not that I'm ashamed of my body. I don't think anyone should be ashamed of their body. But when you are short and rather dumpy, you don't necessarily want to take all your clothes off in front of people. Not even your best friends! And anyway, the Jemima person wasn't a friend. She was a total stranger, and shouldn't have been there.

"Nobody's going nude," said Keri. "Not unless they want to. I've got heaps of spare bathing costumes!"

"Actually," said Frizz, "I don't feel like going swimming anyway."

Keri at once said, "Why not?"

"'Cos I just don't."

When Frizz digs her heels in, there's no budging her. She can be quite stubborn. So she sat on the side and watched, while Keri did her usual showing-off bit, diving and thrashing up and down, and Jemima floated about on her back, in what I can only describe as a *languid* fashion, and Lily did her scrabble paddle and I mostly stayed in the shallow end and talked to Frizz.

"Look, look!" squealed Lily, paddling towards us. "We could do a water ballet!" She put one foot on the bottom and sprang up into the air, flapping her arms like wings.

"What's that supposed to be?" said Frizz.

"Guess!"

We couldn't.

"*Swan Lake!*" cackled Lily.

How were we to know? We're not into ballet. Sometimes I do believe it's all Lily ever thinks about. But that, of course, is why she is one day going to be a Big Star and FAMOUS. She is truly dedicated!

When Keri finally decided that we'd had enough of swimming we all dried ourselves off and went back upstairs to her room. It was still too early for tea, so we sat about on cushions on the floor and talked. I picked at a scab on my knee, and Frizz chewed the end of her plait, and Lily folded herself into peculiar shapes, with her legs all bent at odd angles.

Usually our Saturday meetings are the hugest fun! We gossip about school, and tell each other all the things that have been happening in our lives. We try on clothes and make-up, and do different hair styles, and have a bit of a giggle. Nothing specially special: just the four of us together, being friends. We've known each other for so long that we don't ever have to pretend, or try to impress. We can just relax and enjoy ourselves!

It wasn't the same, with a stranger. The Jemima person was so LOUD, and so CLANGY. She kept shrieking and going, "Yah!" And she and Keri did nothing but talk about this school they both go to, this boarding school called Nathan House where Keri stays during the week.

Keri would say, "God, I hope we're both in Primrose!"

To which the Jemima person would reply, "God, so do I!" at the top of her voice.

"I shall just *die* if I'm with the Dork!"

"I shall die if I'm in Bluebell!"

"Me, too! I shall *die*!"

And then, very kindly, Keri would condescend to explain to the rest of us what they were talking about. "Bluebell and Primrose are two of our dorms. The others are called Daffodil and Hyacinth."

"Hyacinth is the *pits*."

"Yes, and they put all the saddos in Bluebell."

"All the geeks."

"Primrose is way the best! Me and Mima were in Primrose last term with two of our friends."

"Alice and Joanna. They're such sweeties."

Yuck.

"And Mrs Huxtable was our form mistress. Oh, God, I hope she still is!"

"God, so do I! Imagine if we have Miss Arnold!"

"Miss Arnold is just *so-o-o* strict," said Keri. She rolled her eyes. "She won't ever let me and Mima sit together."

"Our class teacher is really nice," I said. "She lets us sit wherever we want. Just so long as we stay put. She doesn't mind."

"Neither does Mrs Huxtable. It's just Miss Arnold who's mean. She's really got it in for poor Mima. And Mima didn't *do* anything. Well, apart from squatting under the back bench in the science lab scoffing doughnuts when she should have been dissecting frogs!"

Both Keri and Jemima broke out into loud peals of laughter.

"I wouldn't ever dissect frogs," I said. "I think it's cruel."

"They were already dead!" shrieked Jemima.

"God," said Keri, "you don't think we'd dissect them *live*?"

"I don't think you should dissect them at all," I said.

"No, well, Mima didn't." Keri cackled again. "She was too busy filling her face with doughnuts!"

"Get fat if you eat doughnuts," said Lily. She had both legs stuck up in the air and was cycling like mad. "Fat, fat, FAT! I've put on half a kilo over Christmas. I don't know what Miss Diamond will say when she weighs us!"

Lily has this obsession with weight. She's skinny as a pin and has these mad fantasies about getting fat. She's not anorexic or anything, but she won't ever pig out on crisps or chocolate like the rest of us. She is into what Mum calls "healthy eating". Like at her dancing school they're taught all about calories, and how many they need. They mustn't have too many and they mustn't have too few. They mustn't get *fat* and they mustn't get *thin*. Oh, dear! What a business. I couldn't be a dancer. I mean, even if I wasn't round to begin with. I would hate not being able to eat what

I wanted! Life would be so *boring*! But I guess you have to make sacrifices if you want to get anywhere. I would quite like to get somewhere, it's just that I haven't yet fixed on where. But wherever it is, I don't want it to be some place I can't pig out when I feel like it!

"Half a kilo is nothing," said Keri. "Last term we had a dorm feast and we got interrupted in the middle of it and had to jump back into bed with all the grub and this one girl, she just went on eating *all night long*. She'd taken this chocolate cake with her and she scoffed the lot and when she woke up in the morning she was like this" – Keri made big balloon shapes in the air. "Her name's Pandora Holicraft. Mima calls her Hovercraft!"

"I shall be a hovercraft if I don't stop eating," said Lily.

"You'll be as skinny as a piece of string," said Keri. "You'll go down the plug hole if you're not careful!"

"It's not good to be too thin." That was the Jemima person again. Daring to lay down the law. To Lily!

"She has to be thin," I said. "She's a dancer."

"I said, *too* thin."

Cheek! Coming into our group and telling Lily she was too thin! I thought this Jemima had pretty much of a nerve, if you want to know. But Keri actually jumped in to support her.

"Mima had a cousin," she said, "that died of being thin."

Even more cheek! Supporting an *outsider*. Lily didn't seem to care; she just went on bicycling.

Unlike me and Frizz, who are full of doubts and fears, Lily is really a very confident sort of person. She doesn't throw her weight around like Keri, but she is always very sure of where she is going and what she is doing. It takes a LOT to rattle her. I wish I could be like that!

"If anybody gets too thin," she said, "they're put on report and sent to the doctor. They're very strict about eating, at our school."

"Mima's cousin got so thin that in the end she was nothing but skin and bone," said Keri. "You could practically see right through her. Couldn't you?"

Jemima nodded. "Right through her."

There was a silence. Lily stopped bicycling and locked her legs behind her head. I picked some more at my scab.

Suddenly, into the silence, came Frizz's voice: "Who's Mima?"

The Jemima person gave this shrill peal of clacking

laughter, like a hen with hiccups. "Yuk yuk clack cackle yuk!"

Keri said, "Je-*mima.*"

"Her," I said, pointing.

"Oh." Frizz turned slightly pink and went back to chewing on her plait. But really, I ask you! Who on earth is called Mima?

At five o'clock Frizzle's dad came to pick us up. He picked Lily up, as well, and we all sat in the back and chatted about the meeting. Even Lily agreed it hadn't been one of the best.

"It was having that Mima there," I said.

"It ruined the mix," said Frizz.

Lily chuckled. "You make it sound like we were baking a cake!"

Earnestly, Frizz said, "It's exactly the same." Frizz is into cooking in a big way. She's good at it! "You only have to just change one ingredient and it can ruin the whole thing."

"Mm." Lily forked a finger into her fringe. "I s'ppose."

"Well, not to worry," I said. "She won't be there next week."

"She shouldn't have been there this week," said Frizz. "Not at one of our meetings."

Frizz quite often comes out and says these things that I would like to say but feel that I shouldn't. I mean, there weren't any rules about not bringing other people to our meetings, and it did seem a bit – well! – small-minded, I suppose. Like having clubs that are men-only, or saying we don't want foreigners to come and live in our country. That sort of thing. But all the same, I agreed with Frizz. That Jemima person shouldn't have been there.

"They're *our* meetings," said Frizz. "Gang of Four. Not for other people!"

"Mm." Lily forked again at her fringe. "I s'ppose."

"Well, they are," insisted Frizz. "If we're going to start bringing other people we won't *be* the Gang of Four!"

Things seemed to be getting a bit heavy. Brightly, to change the subject, I said, "School on Monday! Who's looking forward to it?"

"Me!" Lily bounced on the seat. "I can't wait! We're going to start *pas de deux* classes."

"What's that?" I said.

"Working with a partner…it'll be ever such fun!"

"We're going to start Latin," I said.

Both Lily and Frizz screwed up their faces.

"Boffin," said Frizz.

I said, "I'm not a boffin!" I hate it when she calls

me that. "I just think it'll be interesting. Anyway, what about you?"

"I'm not doing Latin!" said Frizz.

"No, I mean…do you mind having to go back?"

Last term Frizz had been really miserable at Heathfield. There were these two girls that had been at Juniors with us and had just been so mean to her, not letting her join their gang that they'd got going. It had really upset Frizz. I was hoping this term she'd be a bit happier.

"What sort of cooking are you going to be doing?" I said.

Frizz said, "Might not be doing cooking. Might be doing something else."

"Like what?" I said. But Frizz just said she didn't know.

When I got home, Mum asked how the meeting had gone. I told her that it had gone OK. "Except that Keri had this friend there. The one at the party. Je-*mima*. She kept going" – I put on this drooly drawly sort of voice – "*Yaaah* and *cooool* and *grrrooooovy!*"

"You didn't get on?" said Mum.

"She didn't fit in," I said. "She's not one of us. Frizz said she spoilt the mix."

"Oh, Polly!" Mum looked at me, reproachfully.

"I do wish you'd stop calling her Frizz! Don't you think it's about time you started to use her real name?"

"No!" I said. "She's Frizz. She's always been Frizz!"

"Yes, and the older she gets," said Mum, "the more tiresome she's going to find it. You can grow out of nicknames, you know."

"Did you ever have one?" I said.

"Not telling you."

"Mum! Please! Did you?"

"I might have done."

"What was it?"

"If you must know," said Mum, "it was Pancake." I said, "*Pancake?*"

"As in, *flat as*," said Mum. "Flat as a pancake. Believe it or not, I was in those days."

I giggled. Mum is anything but flat now! I was the one that was flat. I hoped nobody started calling me Pancake!

"You can laugh," said Mum. "It wasn't funny even at the time, and it was even less funny as I grew older. I don't expect it's very funny for Dawn, either."

"She doesn't mind," I said.

"How do you know?" said Mum. "Have you ever asked her?"

I admitted that I hadn't. "But we've always called her Frizz!"

"That is no argument," said Mum. "You just try asking her, and see what she says."

I promised that I would. "Next time we meet…I'll do it. Just for you!"

"Thank you," said Mum.

Chapter 3

On Monday, we went back to school.
I made an entry in my nice new diary.

MONDAY
Beginning of spring term. Got all my
clothes ready last night and hung them
over the back of a chair. Also packed my bag.
Mum most impressed! Said she didn't know
what had come over me. She is not used
to me being so efficient!!! (But it is my
New Year's resolution.)

I set my alarm for seven o'clock that day and left for school really EARLY as I was terrified of being late, like I had been at the start of last term. As a result I got there before anyone else and was able to bag a seat for Chloë. At the back, in the corner! I also bagged ones for Chantal and Katie (next to us) and Bev and Susha (in front). Jessamy Jones, our arch enemy, was nowhere near! Nobody thought to save a seat for her. She was really put out, you could tell, but it served her right for being so pushy all the time. I had the feeling people were beginning to get really fed up with her, just like we did at Juniors.

Lettice – the girl that had tried to latch on to me last term – had now latched on to a poor innocent person called Joyce that was new to the school, having just arrived from Hong Kong. She seemed very nice and totally harmless so that I felt quite sorry for her. I know what it is like when Lettice latches on! She won't let you be friends with anyone else and even resents it if you just try talking to them. Susha, that she latched on to after she'd latched on to me, was now friends with Bev and I was glad about that as Susha is a really sweet person.

Nobody was friends with Jessamy and I was glad about that as well! Jessamy is anything *but* sweet. She still hung out with us at break time, however. There just seemed no way we could get rid of her. She even tried to tell us what to do, but we didn't do it. No way! Chloë said she spent all last term being shoved around by Jessamy and she wasn't going to put up with it any more. Me neither! She is even worse than Keri. At least Keri is *fun*. I know I sometimes get bolshy with her but that is just a matter of principle. She always has good ideas for things to do and places to go. Jessamy is just – well – bossy!

We still had Mrs Pollard as class teacher. Hooray! Mrs Pollard also takes us for English, which is way my best subject, so this means we have a *good relationship*. Unlike with Mrs Burkett, for example, who is Maths. Mrs Burkett says that she despairs of me. She is not the only one! Dad also despairs of me. He says that there he is, working out all the huge volumes of water that will be needed to go into people's swimming pools, and I cannot even work out how much wallpaper would be needed to paper a room! Which is what we did in Maths that first day back and Mrs Burkett said that if I bought all that amount of paper I would be able to decorate the whole of Buckingham Palace, practically. Better too much than too little, is what I say! But in any case I am not going to paper rooms. If ever I have a house of my own I will just paint it, in bright colours, and maybe do murals. I think that would be fun!

I so much enjoyed writing in my diary that I went on writing all the rest of that week.

TUESDAY
We have started Latin! (I wrote)
I think I am going to like it.

For our first lesson we just learnt words, like for instance:
Puella (a girl)
Puer (a boy)
Canis (a dog)
Equus (a horse)

Dad says that he thinks Latin is a waste of time. He reckons it would be of far more use if I could work out how many rolls of paper it would take to paper a room rather than being able to say, "This is a table" or "Here is a horse", but I think it is interesting! (I do not think papering a room is interesting. I think it is hard work and messy.)

Latin has turned out to be one of my favourite subjects!

WEDNESDAY
Rang Frizz when I got in from school.
Asked her how she was getting on and
she said, "OK", sounding quite cheerful.

I was relieved to hear Frizz being cheerful as I don't like it when she is unhappy. But that evening, three cheers! She was all enthusiastic and said that they were still doing cooking in Home Ec. She said, "We're doing cordon vert!"

I said, "Don't you mean cordon bleu?" thinking to myself that languages have never been Frizz's best subject, but she said no, she meant cordon vert. She said, "Don't you know what it is?"

I said, "Obviously something green", (showing off my knowledge of French).

"It's *vegetarian*," said Frizz. She was all triumphant about it, 'cos of knowing something I didn't. I suppose I was being a bit boffinish. I asked her why it was called green, but she didn't seem to have any answer to that. She said, "It just is." She promised that she would cook something to bring with her on Saturday.

She said, "Tell your mum!"

So I said to Mum that Frizz was going to bring something cordon vert for our tea, "So you won't have to bother getting anything."

Mum said, "Something veggie. Good! That should be better than all the junk food you normally stuff yourself with... Chocolate bars and crisps and chips-with-everything!"

I pointed out to Mum that in fact chocolate bars and crisps, and chips as well, for that matter, are all vegetarian. I said, "They are cordon vert."

"They may be vegetarian," said Mum. "I don't know about cordon vert!"

I said, "Why *vert*, anyway? Why green?"

"Because it's healthy," said Mum. "Good for you, good for the planet...did you ask Dawn, by the way?"

I said, "Ask her what?"

Mum tutted and said that my memory was alarmingly poor for one so young. "About being called by that ridiculous nickname!" she said.

I reminded her that in fact I had promised to do it *when we met.* "So it's your memory that's poor," I said, "not mine!"

"Ah, yes, but I have an excuse," said Mum. "I'm

not eleven years old."

All I would say to that, I wrote in my diary, *is huh!*

THURSDAY
Now I am saying it again (I wrote).
Huh huh HUH! Only this time I am
not saying it about Mum but about
Jessamy Jones. Honestly! That girl!

She was standing in the classroom that morning, all puffed up and self-important, pinning stuff on the bulletin board. Something about subs being due for the camera club, her being our class representative. All of a sudden she drops a pin – just as I happen to be on my way past. So guess what? She has the nerve to turn and flap this languid hand (I love that word! – *languid*) and in her best imitation of the Queen giving orders she goes, "Polly, just pick that up."

No *please* or *would you mind* or *could you possibly*. Just, *pick that up*.

Well! I had no intention of doing so. Not after that. Not even if she went on her bended knees and begged me. She glowered down at me and snapped, "Polly! Did you hear what I said? I asked you to pick it up!"

I said, "Call that asking? Sounded more like an order to me."

"So why not obey it?" she says.

"'Cos I don't feel like it," I say.

Dad would have accused me of being bolshy. Which probably I was! But she just gets me so mad.

"Look, are you going to pick up that pin or not?" she goes.

And I go, "No, as a matter of fact! I'm not."

So then she gives me this long hard stare, like I'm a bunch of snot someone's just blown out of their nose, and says, "In that case, all I can say is that you are obviously a very nasty little girl."

Cheek! I told Chloë about it and, for some reason, she found it funny. All the rest of the day she kept saying to me: "You are obviously a *very nasty* little girl." Which made us both giggle!

FRIDAY
Have arranged to see Chloë out
of school! Not this weekend but next.
I am looking forward to it!

Chloë and I had never met out of school before. How it happened, Chloë said to me that morning, "Are you

47

still seeing your friends on Saturdays?" I told her that I was and I could see she was disappointed. Like she'd thought it would be fun if her and me could do things on Saturdays. Which it would, but as I explained to her, "We made this vow, to stay in touch."

"*Every Saturday!*" said Chloë.

"Well...yes," I told her. I almost said why didn't she come along. I was really tempted! After all, if that great shrieking Mima could come, I didn't see any reason Chloë shouldn't. But then I thought of Frizz, and how it might upset her, I mean what with her being my oldest friend and all. And I did agree about outsiders spoiling the mix. At the same time, I wanted so much for Chloë to come round, and to see my bedroom and all my things, and to meet Bundle. Chloë wanted it, too. She said, "What about Sunday?" So that is what we arranged, and I wrote it down in big letters in my diary:

CHLOË, 11 o'clock. To walk Bundle.

It was a whole week away and I didn't want to forget. I was positive I wouldn't, but Mum had bought me my diary specially to write my engagements in. It made me feel very well-organised and efficient!

Like just imagine if someone should want to see me that Sunday, I would be able to say, "Excuse me one moment while I consult my diary." And then, "I'm so sorry! I am otherwise engaged on that date." Or even, maybe, if my life got *really* hectic: "I'm afraid I'm fully booked up till the end of the year." Ho ho! A likely tale, as Craig would say.

SATURDAY
Gang of Four meeting, at my house.
This meeting was one of the best
ones we have ever had!

This was what I wrote in my diary. And it was, too! It was a really, really good meeting. So much so that I felt quite sad that I hadn't invited Chloë, though probably it had been wisest not to. We had *such* fun, and she might have been like Jemima and spoilt the mix. And then it would have been all my fault!

Frizz turned up first, with her veggie food that she had done. A big pot of...something or other!

I asked her what it was and she beamed and said, "Goulash! Without the meat." Then she lifted the lid and told me to have a sniff. I quivered my nose over the top of it, and it did smell quite scrummy. Mum said she would put it in the oven to keep warm until we were ready to eat it. "Dawn is becoming quite a chef!" she said. And she gave me this Meaningful Glance. But I hadn't forgotten! I had every intention of keeping my promise, I was just waiting for the right moment.

Keri and Lily arrived soon after Frizz. They came in Keri's mum's car, with a great suitcase full of old clothes that Keri's grandma had given her. All from the sixties and seventies, when she was young.

"She was going to sell them," said Keri. "You can get a lot of money for stuff like this. But then she gave them to me instead! Look!"

She threw open the lid of the suitcase and we all squealed. It was like a treasure trove! Keri announced that we were going to get dressed up and have a fashion parade, and for once I wasn't bolshy. I couldn't wait to get started!

Before she would let us choose what clothes we were going to wear Keri said we had to get made up. "Proper 60s make-up." She said we'd all got to have panda eyes. Frizz wanted to know what panda eyes were. So did I! Keri said it was when people went to bed without bothering to take their make-up off and when they woke up in the morning they looked like pandas, with big black rings round their eyes. She said they went round like it all the time, and she made us up with thick black eye liner and turned our eyelashes into spiders' legs, all black and hairy. Then we painted rouge on our cheeks and did our lips bright red.

Lily took one look at me and screeched. "You look like someone's cut a great gash in your face!"

"So do you," I said.

Lily looked at herself in the mirror and screeched again. "Way out!"

"It was the height of fashion in those days," said Keri. "I've seen pictures... It's how our grans used to look."

It is very strange, trying to imagine your grans being young, with panda eyes and spiders' legs and teensy little miniskirts showing all their legs!

Lily put on a miniskirt, but she is so tiny that it reached right down past her knees. Keri said, "Fold it in half!" So she did, and then it hardly even covered her bum, but that was all right because Lily's bum is really cute from all the dancing that she does. Unlike mine, which tends to be – ahem – excuse me – a bit *squishy*. "Like two ferrets fighting in a bag," is what Craig says. Boys are just so horrible!

Keri also put on a miniskirt. She looked a-MAZING!

Like she was about eighteen. I told her that she had better not go out like that and she struck this pose, all flirty, pouting her lips, and said, "Dare me?" Which I didn't, because if I had she might actually have gone and done it, and I didn't think Mum would be best pleased. She always says Keri is a bit too cool for her own good. "Eleven going on twenty-one," is the way Mum puts it. I sometimes think Mum would like us all to stay eleven going on nine!

I didn't fancy the idea of a miniskirt as I think you have to have the right legs, which I haven't. So I found a pair of dungarees that when I got into them were so huge I could practically walk around inside them! Then I found a really groovy cap, red velvet with a big peak and a little pompom on top. The peak fell down over my nose!

Lily went, "Aaaah! Sweet!"

Keri said the dungarees were a killer. "You could share them with the rest of us... We could all get in there with you!"

Frizz had discovered a pair of jeans that flared out at the bottom like a big skirt, so that when we looked at her we all burst out laughing. Keri snatched up her camera and said, "Let me take a picture!" but Frizz wouldn't, not even when she snapped Lily in her mini strip and me in my baggy dungarees. Frizz said, "No! It looks stupid!"

"But I've got to have one of all of us," said Keri. She handed the camera to Lily, "Here! Take one of me."

In the meanwhile, I had been rootling about in the suitcase and came up with...a suspender belt! *Pink*. And frilly.

"Hey! Sexy!" cried Keri. "Frizz, give it a go!"

I thought Frizz would be too shy, but she immediately pulled off the jeans and put on the suspender belt, and a pair of stockings that went with it – black and fishnetty. Dead cool! – plus a pair of shoes with long spiky heels about three inches tall. She then paraded about the room, while we all giggled like crazy and Keri went snap, snap, snap with her camera.

We had one moment of panic when someone knocked on the door and we thought it was Mum and said, "Come in", and it turned out to be Craig. His mouth didn't half drop open at the sight of Frizz in her suspender belt!

"Get out!" I said. "What are you doing?"

Craig said, "What are *you* doing?"

It was Frizz who told him we were having a fashion

show and that "Boys are not allowed". I was well surprised! Normally she would have been covered in embarrassment! Frizz, it seemed, had hidden depths! Craig was the one who was embarrassed. I thought, tee hee! That would teach him.

After tea, when we all ate Frizz's goulash, which was ace, and Keri and Lily had been collected by Keri's dad, I remembered my promise to Mum. I asked Frizz whether she minded us calling her Frizz. She said, "I don't mind you calling me Frizz. But I wouldn't want to be called Frizz in public!"

I asked her what she meant by "in public". Frizz said, "Well – you know!" And then she went a bit pink. "If ever I was in the papers or anything," she mumbled.

I wondered why Frizz thought that she was ever likely to be in the papers. I mean, Lily might be. Keri might be. But not Frizz! Not me, either, if it comes to that.

I said, "We could stop if you like. It's only because of your surname." Frizzell. Pronounced Frizelle. (As she is forever telling us!) "We could always call you Dawn, if you'd rather."

But Frizz pulled a face and said she didn't think Dawn was all that much better than Frizz. She said, "I wish they could have christened me something romantic like Miranda."

I had to try really hard not to giggle when she said this. I mean, Frizz just is not a Miranda type of person. But it just goes to show that we all have our secret daydreams! Mine being that I could have green eyes and long legs and be called Jade...

Dream on!

That Saturday was the last real entry that I ever made in my lovely new diary. I still wrote down my social engagements (when I had any!) and special events like birthdays. And because it seemed a shame to waste all the beautiful blank pages I made out a few lists, like Top Tens of music and books and TV progs, etc. I also made a wish list.

What I wish for the Future:
That Mum would let me wear contact lenses
(green ones) instead of glasses.
That I could come top of English.
That I could grow TALL.
That I could be SLIM.
That I could change my name to Jade.
That the world could be a better place.

I put that last one in as I felt it was the sort of thing

that any right-minded person ought to wish for, and in case in years to come someone might discover my diary and think, "Ho! This Polly Roberts must have been a very shallow kind of person." Which is what they probably would think if my wishes were all as trivial and self-centred as having green contact lenses and being called Jade. I do *try* to have a wider view of life.

Anyway, that was the end of my diary-keeping. Most of the pages after that are full of meaningless doodles and squiggles and bits of poetry that I felt inspired to compose. But I didn't ever go back to making proper entries. Life was just too full to keep writing it all down!

Chapter 2

These are just some of the things that life was full of:

Schoolwork (especially French, Latin and English!)
Taking Bundle for walks
Quarrelling with Craig
Going back with Chloë for tea
Chloë coming back with me for tea
Going to parties (I was invited to three!)
And, of course,
Our Saturday meetings.

It is just as well I am a person that enjoys work because at school our timetables were absolutely crammed. It was all rush, rush, rush from one class to the next, carting great armfuls of books as we went.

When I told Frizz about it – not complaining; just telling – she said that was what came of going to a boffin school, so that I immediately wished I hadn't mentioned it. I'd just thought it was funny, the corridors full of people frantically racing this way and that, and prefects standing in the middle waving their arms and shouting, "No running! Single file!"

"Don't you have that at Heathfield?" I said.

Frizz said no. "People just barge."

"But don't you get into trouble?"

"Only if you bash into a teacher," said Frizz.

I said, "Heavens! We get given order marks just for *jostling*, practically."

"We sometimes get traffic jams," said Frizz. "Like if a crowd of boys all try to get through a door at the same time and get stuck."

"Then what happens?" I said.

"You just have to wait till they get unstuck," said Frizz.

"Really? I couldn't imagine people getting stuck in doorways at the High School!"

"Well, or until the caretaker comes along," said Frizz.

"What does he do?"

"He *boots* them!" Frizz cackled and kicked out with a foot. "Boots them up the backside!"

I looked at her, dubiously. Could this be true? Or was she just pulling my leg? Sometimes, with Frizz, you just don't know.

"We don't have anything like that," I said.

"Course you don't," said Frizz. "It's too posh, where you go."

I wish she wouldn't say things like that! I pointed out to her that I wasn't posh, I'd had to get a scholarship. "My mum and dad couldn't ever have afforded to pay."

"Yes, well, you're a boffin," said Frizz. "And anyway," she added, "you don't have boys."

At the High School, she meant. It is strictly all-girls, and a good thing too, if you ask me! Boys are just so *boring*. Boys are boring, girls are groovy. I said this to Frizz. "Don't you think so?" I said.

"Oh, they're all right," said Frizz. "They're just...boys. They can't help it."

Of course they can't *help it*. Nobody can help how they're born. A hyena can't help being born a hyena: boys can't help being born boys. But I was still glad I didn't have to go to school with them! It was bad enough having one for a brother. Me and Craig just seemed to quarrel all the time. It's funny, 'cos we never did when we were younger. Not seriously. But all of a sudden it just seemed like we were from different planets. Everything he did annoyed me and everything I did annoyed him. I told him that boys were slime. He said that girls sucked.

Mum said she was sick to death of the pair of us. "I'm sick of the sound of your voices!"

Dad said if we didn't stop it he would knock our heads together, whereupon Craig got cheeky and told Dad he wasn't allowed to do that. "It's against the law, to whack your children. They could put you in prison for that."

"So they can put me in prison!" roared Dad.

I don't know if we'd still have quarrelled if we'd both been girls. Or – hideous thought! – both been boys. Gran said it was just a phase we were going through. "They'll grow out of it."

Mum said, "Yes, but not before they've driven me stark mad!" She said if there was much more of it she would end up on the streets in a black plastic bin bag with a banana stuck in her ear.

I told this to Chloë and we had a giggle about it. Me and Chloë giggled about lots of things! Mum in her bin bag, Jessamy calling me a nasty little girl, the

Heathfield caretaker booting boys up the backside.

"Imagine Mr Terkel," I said. Mr Terkel is our caretaker at the High School. He is very tall and skinny with big knobbly hands and long splatty feet. Really good for booting!

"Imagine Jessamy," gurgled Chloë.

Jessamy in a doorway, being booted up the bottom by Mr Terkel with his long splatty feet... It made us giggle so much we both got stomach pains!

During the week, while I was at school, it was Chloë who was my best friend; but out of school it was still Frizz. It would always be Frizz! Just like it would always be the Gang of Four. Even when we were old and withered.

"We'll still meet up," said Lily. "We'll hobble there with our Zimmer frames!" And she hunched up her shoulders and became an old person, slowly shuffling across the room with her Zimmer.

"Not me!" declared Keri.

Frizz looked at her, reproachfully. "You mean, you won't still want to meet?"

"Not with a Zimmer frame! I shall get cabs everywhere. Or have a Rolls Royce, with a chauffeur!" She probably will, too. Knowing Keri.

"So long as you still come," said Frizz.

"Course I'll still come! We swore an oath, didn't we?"

We'd sworn FOR EVER. And our last few meetings had been really good! We hadn't had any more fashion parades, but what we'd done, we'd sat and talked like we hadn't talked since being at Juniors. Last term had been a bit bumpy, what with Frizz being miserable, and Lily having to miss meetings because of special dance classes, and Keri simply not turning up, and me getting in a muddle with my social engagements.

This term we were all more settled. Frizz had palled up with a girl in her class called Marigold, which meant she wasn't on her own any more. I had Chloë, Keri had Mima. Lily hadn't teamed up with anyone in particular but she is one of those people who is always popular. I mean, everyone just always loves Lily! So it wasn't like she was short of friends, or anything.

As well as being settled, we were all busy! Lily was doing her *pas de deux* work, Frizz was doing her cooking, I was learning Latin – *mensa,* a table, and *frater*, a brother. "Fatuous frater!" I called Craig when I wanted to get my own back. As for Keri, she was in the netball team, and the hockey team, and the fencing team, and the swimming team. She was in practically every team there was going! So we all had loads to talk about.

Every meeting there would be something new and exciting.

"Hey, you guys! Guess what?" That would be Keri, bouncing through the door. "I made the team!" The hockey team. The netball team. The fencing team. "I'm actually *in*!"

And then, the following week: "I've got a part! I've got a part!" That would be Lily, jubilantly prancing round the room. "I've been picked for the end of term show! I've got a real proper part! I'm a dragonfly!"

And then it would be my turn, telling how I'd been voted Year Seven representative for the school magazine. "*Me!* I just can hardly believe it!"

"Why not?" said Keri. "You've always come top of English."

"Yes, I know," I said. "But there's this girl in Nightingale, Alice Marshall, she's really popular. I really thought she'd be the one!"

"She might be *popular*," said Keri, "but that doesn't mean she's good at English."

"She is!" I said. "She won a prize!"

"Bet she's not as good as you," said Frizz.

"No, 'cos d'you remember that poem you wrote?" Lily took hold of one of her legs and just casually bent it up behind her. She is always doing this sort of thing. She does it without even thinking. "Back in Year Five? Poem about Bundle? *My dog Bundle, loves to trundle*."

"Don't!" I clapped both my hands to my cheeks. "I can't bear it!"

"It was a good poem," said Lily. "How did it go? My dog Bundle—"

"I can't remember!"

"Something about walking round the park."

I said,

"My dog Bundle, loves to trundle
All about the park."

"Yes! And then there was a bit about him barking."

"He loves to spring, he loves to swim,
He loves to have a bark."

"See!" Lily lowered her leg, exultantly. "It was good!"

"It was all right," I said. "But that was in Year Five. I've moved on since then."

Frizz said, "Yes! So've I. I g—"

"I've got to write another one," I said.

"I got t—"

"A *new* one. For the magazine."

"I got t—"

"I can't think what to write it about!"

"Top marks," said Frizz.

"What?" Keri swished with an imaginary hockey stick. "Top marks in what?"

"Cookery," said Frizz.

"Really?" said Keri. "That's brilliant!"

I was going to ask Frizz what she'd cooked, but Keri had already gone rattling on. "I've got to practise like mad! We've got a really big match next week."

"I've got to go to extra rehearsals,' said Lily. "They put it on the board yesterday…extra rehearsals, twice a week."

I said, "Not on a Saturday, I hope?"

"No. Tuesdays and Thursdays, after school. There's five of us… Dragonfly, Butterfly" – Lily counted them off on her fingers – "Moth, Bee, Ladybird. Look! These are some of the steps that I do."

Lily leapt on to the bed (it was her own bed), stood for a moment with her arms held stiff and straight by her sides, fingers all spiky, then suddenly sprang into life, zigzagging across the room in a series of sharp little steps. It took us by surprise! Frizz rolled sideways, thinking Lily was going to land on her, but Lily simply jumped right over.

"That's how it starts," she said. "I haven't learnt the rest yet. Of course I can't do it properly in here, there's not enough room. When I'm on stage I *skim*" – she took a flying leap back on to the bed – "from here to there! And I'm going to have this really *bright* costume, all reds and greens and purple, with sequins and shiny stuff. And *wings!* I'm so glad I'm a dragonfly," cried Lily, soaring down again off the bed, "and not a bee! Bees just bumble" – she did a little bumbly hop – "and buzz...bzzzzzzzzzzzzz!" she went, into Frizz's face.

"Yes. Well," said Keri. "That all looks very exhausting. Almost as exhausting a playing in a hockey match."

"More!" Lily kicked out with a leg. "I'm on stage the *whole time*, and I've got this solo where I *dart*" – she darted (at Keri, who didn't flinch) – "and *zoom*" – she zoomed (at me, who did) – "all about the stage, up and down, in and out, round about...oops!" said Lily, crashing into the edge of a cupboard. "I told you I couldn't do it properly in here!"

On the way home Frizz said to me, "You don't think Lily's getting to be a luvvy, do you?"

I thought about it a bit. "No," I said. "I don't think so. I think she's just excited. 'Cos it is exciting, isn't it?

When you get chosen for things?"

"You don't have to show off about it," said Frizz.

It hadn't occurred to me that Lily was showing off. I didn't think she was; not really.

"I think she just wanted to share it with us," I said. "I mean, that's what friends are for. If you can't tell your friends your good news, who can you tell?

I said this to Frizz, and she said, "Mm…maybe." She didn't sound terribly convinced.

"Well, anyway," I said, "I've got to go and write my poem. I'll read it to you next week!"

I didn't actually *have* to write a poem. I could have written an article or a short story. But I like doing poems best! Even when I can't think of anything to do them about… I never let a little thing like that bother me! I just go ahead and write.

Next week, when we met at Frizz's place, I had my poem all ready and waiting.

"Do you want to hear it?" I said.

"Yes!" Lily couldn't nod because she was standing on her head at the time. But she waggled a foot, to encourage me.

"Right." I cleared my throat. "Are you ready?"

"Just get on with it," said Keri. "The suspense is killing me!"

I opened my mouth to begin. "Poem. By P—"

"I think we all ought to be sitting properly," said Frizz.

"Oh! Yes. Sitting properly." Lily came down off her head and rearranged herself in a sitting position. She beamed at me. "Now you can start!"

"*Poem*." I said. "By Polly Roberts. Year Seven, Brontë." Brontë is the house that I am in.

"I'm trying to write a good poem
To go in the school magazine.
But I can't seem to think of a subject –
My muse is not to be seen!
I—"

"Your what?" said Frizz.

"My *muse*," I said.

"Her muse," said Keri.

"I'll start again." I said.

"I'm trying to write a good poem
To—"

"What's a muse?" said Frizz.

"A thing that gives you inspiration!" I'm afraid I snapped it, rather. I really hate it when people keep interrupting! "I'll start *again*.

I'm—"

"Like in amuse?" said Frizz. "Like something funny?"

"Or like in meee-*ew*," said Lily. "Mee-ew, mee-ew!" Lily started making catty noises and pretending to rub her whiskers. Frizz immediately joined in. "Mee-ew, mee-ew!"

They can be so childish at times. It's really pathetic.

"Look here!" shouted Keri. "This isn't fair! We didn't do this to you when you were dancing! Just shut up and listen!"

Surprise, surprise. They did! There wasn't another squeak out of either of them till I'd finished.

"And so at last we've reached the close.

But what it's about, I think nobody knows!"

"That was fun," said Lily. "I liked that!"

"So did I," said Frizz. "I hope they put it in."

"Oh, it's going to be *in*," I said. "I'm on the committee!"

"I'm in a c—" began Frizz.

"What committee?" said Keri.

"*Editorial* committee. Wh—"

"How did you get to be on that?"

"I was elected," I said. "We all had to vote, and I got voted in! What were you saying?" I said to Frizz.

"Oh, nothing," said Frizz.

"I thought you were going to say something."

"Wasn't important."

"Oh, come on!" cried Lily. "Tell!"

Frizz had turned very pink. "It's not important. It doesn't matter."

Well! You can't make someone talk if they don't want to.

"We're having a committee meeting on Monday," I said. "That's when we'll decide which pieces to choose."

Next Saturday I was able to report that my poem was being given pride of place: "It's going on the very first page!"

"Oh, this is so great!" cried Keri. "Everything's happening all at once!" And she told us excitedly how she had scored three goals in her hockey match and had her name read out in morning assembly.

"And I," announced Lily, "have been moved into Madame Assante's class for classical ballet!"

This might not have meant much to the rest of us, but it obviously meant a lot to Lily. She said that everybody, but *everybody*, wanted to work with Madame Assante. "She is just the BEST!"

And so it went on, every week something new. Life was just so full! And then one week Keri announced that she had something *really* important to tell us.

"But I mean *really*!"

"What, what?" We gathered round, all eager to hear.

In solemn tones, Keri said: "I've started."

She meant, of course, that she had started her periods. Wow! We naturally all wanted to know when, and how, and what it was like.

Keri said it wasn't like anything, really. "I mean, it's no big deal." Now that she'd told us, she could afford to be cool about it. "It's just something that happens. You'll find out, sooner or later. Some people just develop more slowly than others. It's nothing to worry about. I'm sure it won't be long," gushed Keri. "And hey! Do you remember?" She turned and prodded Frizz in the ribs. "When we were young, you thought it happened to boys!"

"I did *not*," said Frizz, growing very red.

"You did, too!"

"I did not! I just wondered. I was only about *six*," said Frizz.

"Eight! You were eight. I remember! We were all whispering about it in our secret place we used to go to and you said you thought it happened to boys! And we wondered which of us it would happen to first – and it's happened to *me*!"

71

Keri sat back, looking well pleased with herself. And then she had a surprise. We all had a surprise. Frizz said, "Well, that's where you're wrong! 'Cos I started weeks ago. Weeks and *weeks* ago. Before we went back to school. So there!"

There was a startled silence.

"Why didn't you tell us?" I said.

Frizz shrugged, and picked at a loose button on her blouse. "Didn't think you'd be interested."

I was totally gobsmacked. Our English teacher says that gobsmacked is a vulgar expression and should not be used but it is the only thing that describes how I felt. I remembered that day we had gone round to Keri's and Frizz had refused to go in the water. Now I knew why!!! But to think that she had hugged it to herself. All these weeks! Frizz and me weren't supposed to have secrets. We had always told each other everything! I could see that maybe, just maybe, she might have been embarrassed telling the others; but not me. I was her best friend!

I couldn't help wondering what other secrets she had in her life.

Chapter 5

"You could at least have told me," I grumbled.

It was the following Saturday, and me and Frizz were toiling up Cherry Tree Hill on our way to Keri's. Cherry Tree Hill is a long hill. And steep! Usually, either Mum or Dad takes us all the way up there, but today it was Dad and he'd dropped us off at the bottom. All because of Craig, who had to be picked up from a football match. I personally thought he could have waited, but Dad said he was already running late. "In any case," he said, "a good stiff climb...just what you need!"

Frizz pulled a face and I wailed, "*Da-a-a-a-d!*" But

to be honest I didn't really mind as it gave me a chance to be on my own with Frizz. We were hardly ever on our own these days. At Juniors we'd always walked back from school together, but since going to secondary school the only real chats we had were on the phone, which I personally just do not think is the same. I mean, for one thing you never know who might happen to be passing by and hear what you are saying, so you can't ever really say anything too private. Not in our house. Not with Craig about! So really and truly I was quite pleased that Dad had dumped us so unceremoniously at the bottom of the hill, even if it did mean a lot of puffing and blowing and aching legs.

"I would have thought—" I stopped and pressed a hand to my side, 'cos now I had a stitch. "I would have thought you would at least have told me. We are supposed," I reminded her, "to be best friends!"

To which Frizz just made a mumbling sound. Maybe she was simply out of breath. We are not as fit as Lily and Keri! But I wasn't going to let her get away with it.

"It's a big event," I said. Keri might pretend to be all cool and laid back, but that was only after she'd broken the news. She'd been absolutely bursting with self-importance when she'd first arrived. "We promised that we'd tell!"

Frizz had gone a bit red, but she still didn't say anything.

"I would have told *you*," I said. "You'd have been the first one I told!"

"When?" said Frizz.

"What do you mean, when?"

"When would you have told me?"

"As soon as it happened!"

Frizz went on stolidly stomping up the hill. I huffed after her.

"I would!" I said.

Frizz looked at me. "How?"

"Well, I'd have – rung you up, or something."

"On the *phone*? With Craig listening in?"

Last time I'd spoken to Frizz on the phone I'd heard someone picking up the extension in Dad's office. I'd yelled, "Whoever that is, *go away*! I'm talking!" Craig's voice had come yelling back at me. "Keep your knickers on! Stupid old bag. How was I to know?"

"He doesn't usually listen," I muttered. Though it was true, I probably wouldn't have used the phone. I mean, you just never know. It could be Dad who picked up the extension, and then I would be covered in embarrassment. I mean, if we were talking about *that*. "I would have told you at a meeting," I said.

"You mean, you'd have told us all together."

"Well – yes. That's what we promised!"

"So you wouldn't have told me first!"

"Like you didn't tell me first!"

"Don't see how I could." Frizz grabbed a handful of someone's hedge and tore off a bunch of leaves as we trudged past. "Never really see you."

Well, honestly! How could she say such a thing?

"We see each other every Saturday!" I said.

"Yes, but it's all talk. Everyone *talking*."

Talking was what we'd always done. Talking was what we liked best. I'd *thought* it was what we'd liked best.

"Talk, talk, talk!" said Frizz. "And nobody listening."

I said, "We do listen! We'd listen to you if you talked. But how can we listen if you just sit there and don't say anything?"

Frizz frowned and concentrated on her leaves.

"P'raps we ought to do something else for a change," I said. "What d'you think?"

"Could, I s'ppose."

"Like what? What could we do?"

Frizz humped a shoulder.

"Suggest something!"

"I don't know!" Frizz hurled her leaves into the gutter. "Don't keep on!"

"I'm not keeping on! I'm just—"

"You are! You're keeping on!"

I heaved a sigh. There is nothing you can do when Frizz is in one of these moods.

"You're not mad about something, are you?" I said, as we reached Keri's house. Frizz shook her head.

"Are you sure?"

She nodded.

"*Honest?*"

"I said! Didn't I?"

"Well, you're behaving in a very weird way," I told her.

I had this feeling that she wasn't really saying what she meant. Something had obviously upset her. Why couldn't she just come straight out with it? I would! But Frizz is funny like that. What Frizz does, she tends to bottle herself up. Like she puts a stopper in her mouth and won't talk. It's kind of maddening, because how can you put things right if you don't even know what's wrong? It's horrid when things go wrong! Especially when you can't work out why.

I didn't have time to question her any more as we were already at Keri's. Lily had got there before us and was already in the pool. We joined her and all splashed about for a bit, then dried ourselves off and went up to Keri's room to eat crisps and drink Coke and to talk. Keri and me and Frizz ate crisps. Lily wouldn't, because of calories, so she cavorted about while we sat and munched and exchanged our usual gossip.

Lily had started her classes with Madame Assante and wanted to share it with us. "She is *so* brilliant! She really inspires you. You just feel you would dance your feet to the bone for her! Some people are frightened of her 'cos she's, like, really fierce, you know? And if she doesn't think you're any good she just sends you to the back of the class and totally ignores you, which is even worse than when she shouts and pokes you with her cane! 'Cos at least if she shouts at you, you know she's noticed you. I mean, she feels you're worth shouting at. You know?"

"Yah. Sure," said Keri; and I nodded, though a bit dubiously. I wasn't certain that I would like to be shouted at.

"I think that sounds horrid," said Frizz.

Lily and Keri both looked at her. "What does?"

"Being shouted at." Frizz is quite bold at times. She comes out with these things. "I don't think there's any need to shout at people."

"It's because she's such a perfectionist," said Lily, earnestly. "She has these really high standards. My first day in her class she pointed at me with her cane" – Lily flung out an imperious arm. "She said, 'You! Child! What is your name?' I said, 'Lily Stubbs, Madame.' I was like quaking in my shoes, my knee caps were bouncing up and down, I was just so terrified! I thought she was going to tell me to leave."

"So what happened?" said Keri.

"She just kind of narrowed her eyes and went 'Hm!' and afterwards everybody said, 'She's noticed you!' They all seemed to think it was a really good sign only I didn't believe them; I thought they were just being kind to me, trying to cheer me up. You know?"

Keri nodded.

"Then the next day" – Lily faced us, her eyes shining – "the *very next day* she told everyone to stop dancing and watch what I was doing. *Me!*" said Lily. "She wanted *me* to demonstrate!"

I said, "Wow!"

"What did she want you to demonstrate?" said Keri. "Show us!"

Lily never needs a second invitation to start dancing. "*Chassé en avant*...into *arabesque*...then *sauté* into *échappé*..."

We watched as Lily sprang about the room.

"Can you imagine how I felt! Being singled out by Madame Assante! In front of the whole class!"

"That happened to me the other day," I said. "I was told to get up and read out my essay...in front of everyone! I was dead embarrassed."

"Me, too!" said Lily.

"Why embarrassed?" said Keri. "I wouldn't be! It just means you're better than everyone else. There's nothing to be *embarrassed* about. It means," she said to Lily, "that you're going to be a star! So you'd better get used to it. And Polly! When you're a famous writer they'll want to interview you on the telly. You'll have to read out bits of your books!"

I felt my cheeks turn pleasantly pink.

"Is that what I'm going to be?" I said. "A famous writer?"

"Well, I should think so," said Keri. "You're always coming top of English and getting As for your essays. Of course you *may* become Prime Minister or run in the Olympics, but somehow I don't think that's very likely."

I giggled. "Neither do I!"

"What about Keri?" said Lily. "What will you be?"

"I shall just be me," said Keri, grandly.

"Yes, and that will be quite enough," agreed Frizz.

We all stopped and looked at her. It sounded like a put-down... Would she dare?

There was a pause.

"I shall be me, and you will be you," said Keri, not sounding quite so certain of herself as she usually did. "And that," she added, rather grandly, "will be enough for both of us!"

It didn't really mean anything, what Keri had said; but we weren't altogether sure what Frizz had meant, either. She seemed to be speaking in riddles today. There was definitely something up with her.

"Anyway," said Lily, "that's all about us! You haven't told us what you've been doing."

"Haven't been doing anything," mumbled Frizz.

"That's just silly," said Keri. "You must have been doing *something*. Even if it's just breathing. What about your cooking? Aren't you still cooking things? Last term you kept making scrummy puddings for us!"

"That was when we were *doing* puddings," said

Frizz. "We're not doing them any more."

"Oh. Well! You could still cook something. Couldn't you?"

"Could, I s'ppose."

"I think you ought! I mean, if you're not doing anything else."

"Actually," I said, "Frizz was saying on the way here that we ought to be doing things. Together."

"I wasn't," said Frizz. "I didn't mean that! I meant—"

Before she could explain what she'd meant, Keri had gone leaping in. "What sort of things? You mean, like, going places? Going skating? That sort of thing?"

"I didn't say w—"

"*Yes!*" Now it was Lily leaping in. "There's something I'd like us to do!"

"But I never—"

"What?" said Keri.

"I saw it in the paper. Not next week, the week after... There's a Celebration of Dance!"

"I saw that," I said. I'd thought of Lily immediately. "It's all over the borough."

"Yes, and in the town centre on Saturday, there's going to be all these dance sessions. For kids! All through the day, at different times. We could go to one of the afternoon ones."

"You're on!" Keri gave the thumbs-up with both hands, fists clenched. I think she must have seen someone do it on the telly. "And I bags we go ice-skating as well!"

"You go ice-skating every Sunday," said Frizz.

"Yes, but I'd like to go with you guys! It would be fun. You're right," said Keri. "We ought to do more things. Not just stuff indoors, talking."

"Let's all choose," said Lily. "I've chosen dancing, Keri's chosen skating...Polly, what about you?"

I said that I'd like it if we could all go on a sponsored dog walk for our local animal shelter. "It's next Saturday. I didn't think I'd be able to go! Mum says she's too busy to come with me but she won't let me go by myself and Craig's playing football and Dad's working and I would just love to be able to 'cos it's where we got Bundle from! And if you all came I could get the forms and people could sponsor you and we could make simply loads of money for them!"

Keri said, "No prob! That's skating, dancing, walking... Frizz! What about you?"

Frizz said she couldn't think of anything.

"There's got to be *something*," said Lily. "Even if it's just going round the shops!"

We agreed that next week we would go on the sponsored walk; the week after we would do the dancing; and the week after that we would go ice-skating. Keri told Frizz to "think of something for when it's your turn", and Frizz promised she would. But on the way home in the car she said to me that she hadn't really meant we had to do things *all the time.*

"So maybe when it's your turn we could just talk, same as usual," I said. "We could meet at your place and you could cook us something!"

"Or you could, for a change," said Frizz.

At the front of the car, Mum gave this short, sharp laugh.

"That'll be the day!" she said. "Couldn't even cook a boiled egg, this one!"

Frizz looked at me, reproachfully. "You don't even know how to boil an *egg*?"

"Course I do!" I said.

"I have yet to see any evidence of it," said Mum. "Stick her in a kitchen, she'd be lost. I doubt she even knows how to turn the oven on!"

Frizz giggled.

"I'd soon find out," I said.

"You ought to know," said Mum. "It's ridiculous!

Always got your head stuck in a book...can't do anything practical at all."

"Don't they teach you at school?" said Frizz.

I didn't like the way she and Mum were ganging up on me. Loftily I said we didn't have time for stuff like that. "We're too busy doing Latin."

"Don't see much point doing Latin if you don't even know how to turn the oven on," said Frizz.

Mum gave another of her laughs. I was beginning to feel distinctly got at.

"Latin happens to be an extremely good discipline for the mind," I said. This was something that I had read somewhere. "Not many people are allowed to do it. The only ones that are allowed to are the ones in the top language set."

"So what do the others do?"

"Um...well! Some of them do cooking," I said.

I didn't mean to be insulting, or anything. It was just a fact. Some people did Latin, some people did cooking. Some people did metalwork. There wasn't any call for Mum to go looking daggers at me.

She told me off about it as soon as we were on our own. "I thought Dawn was supposed to be your best friend?" she said. "Is that the way you treat your best friend? Boasting, and showing off, and putting her down?"

My cheeks fired up. I hate people that boast! How dare Mum accuse me of it? I said, "I wasn't boasting!"

"Sounded like it to me," said Mum. "I'll tell you what, my girl! It may be all very clever, spouting Latin, but it wouldn't be much help on a desert island!"

"Not going to be on a desert island," I muttered.

"I just hope for your sake that you're not," said Mum. "You'd never survive five minutes!"

I thought Mum was being totally unfair. I would *never* have said about being in the top language set if she and Frizz hadn't ganged up against me. They were the ones who'd started it!

As soon as I got in I rang Frizz up. I wasn't going to apologise 'cos I didn't see why I should. I was the one that ought to be apologised to! All the same, I never meant to quarrel with her. I still don't quite know how it happened. I asked her if she'd thought of anything special that she wanted us to do for when it was her turn to choose, and she said no, and that wasn't what she'd meant anyhow. So I said what *had* she meant, and she said, "Doesn't matter", and from there we got on to her keeping secrets from me, at which point Frizz went into one of her long black silences which is something that drives me *crrrrazy.*

In the end I slammed the receiver back and stamped upstairs in this simply terrific rage.

It was the first time that Frizz and I had ever really fallen out. Seriously, that is. I hated it! Frizz obviously did, too, 'cos half an hour later she rang back. Mum called up to me. "Dawn is on the phone." I went and yelled over the banisters: "I don't want to speak to her!"

"Polly, for goodness' sake," said Mum. "Don't be so childish!"

Me? Why always me? But then I relented, and picked up the phone.

Frizz said, "Polly?"

I said, "Frizz?"

Silence.

"Look, I'm sorry," I said.

"Same here," said Frizz.

"We are still friends," I said, "aren't we?"

"Course we are!" said Frizz.

So it all ended OK. Except that she had still kept secrets from me! I didn't know that I could forgive her for that.

Chapter 6

You will never believe it, but Frizz turned up for our sponsored walk wearing *sandals*.

"We're going cross country!" I shrieked. "Haven't you got any wellies?"

Frizz hung her head." They're too small for me."

"Well, then," I said. "Shoes, or something!"

"I don't see what's wrong with sandals," said Frizz. "They're ever so comfortable, and it hasn't rained for weeks."

"It may not have *rained*," I said, "but the fields are *boggy*." I mean, it was the middle of March, for goodness' sake! Who goes for a country walk in the middle of March wearing *sandals*?

Frizz, that's who. I thought, *trust her!* I told her rather snappishly that if she got her feet wet that was her problem. Mum said that maybe we should turn round and go back and let Frizz put something else on, but Frizz didn't want to do that.

"I'll be all right," she said. "I like wearing sandals."

I decided that there are some people you just can't help. After we'd collected the other two – Keri in green wellies, Lily in trainers – Mum drove out along the river and dropped us off at the starting point. I grumbled to Frizz that even if she couldn't get into her wellies she might at least have worn sensible shoes. Frizz said that the only sensible shoes she'd got were her school ones. "Mum didn't want me to wear those."

"Well, just don't whinge," I said, "if you get covered in mud."

I know I was being mean, but I was still feeling sore about Frizz keeping secrets from me. And she does have a tendency to whinge! She gets all pathetic and sorry for herself. I didn't want her ruining our walk. I'd been sponsored by simply loads of people. If we did the whole first lap, which was five miles, I would make

£32 for the animal shelter! The others had all worked really hard getting sponsors, so between us we would make nearly a hundred, which I think is quite a lot.

Mum had said that she would meet us at the five-mile mark. She didn't mind us going by ourselves 'cos there were simply dozens of other people, all with their dogs. We couldn't possibly get lost!

Bundle goes mad over the fields. It's his ace special walkies. He charges about everywhere. He gets the scent of fox or badger, and that's it, he's off! We mooched along in his wake, gossiping as usual about school and work and all the stuff that we were doing.

Lily told us more about Madame Assante and how she had reduced one girl to tears. "She said she was crashing about like an elephant and what on earth did she think she was doing at a ballet school?"

Keri told us about her latest hockey match: "We beat them by four goals! And now we're in the semi-finals!"

I recited a poem I'd made up, to help me remember my Latin vocabulary:

"My brother is a *puer*
I am a *puella*.
We fight like cat and *canis*
We're always making *bella*!

"See, *bellum* means war," I said. Only I don't know how it goes...*bellum, belli, bello*...something like that. It probably shouldn't be *bella*. It should probably be *belli* or something."

A family walking nearby had been listening to me. They were impressed, you could tell! But then Frizz had to go and ruin it all.

"*Belly?*" she said.

"Well, or something."

"Belly!" said Frizz. ""We're going to fight a belly!"

I said, "*Belli* like in *bellicose*," but she took no notice.

She said, "Off to belly!" and started doing this stupid marching step, squelch, squidge, all through the mud. Lily immediately joined in, and then so did Keri, who I would have thought better of.

"Oh belly, oh bello, oh bella," they chanted, much to the amusement of the family that had been listening.

I had been so proud of my Latin poem! Now I had the feeling they were just making fun of it. They thought I was a boffin. *And it was Frizz who had started it*. I didn't think that was very loyal. Not when she was supposed to be my friend.

I followed them in a bit of a hump until we came

to the last field, which we had to cross to reach Mum and the car. I clipped Bundle on to his lead and opened the gate. Frizz came to a horrified halt. "We're not going in *there*?"

"We've got to," I said.

"But it's got *cows* in it!"

"Cows won't hurt you," I said. I have absolutely no patience with anyone that is scared of a gentle animal like a cow.

I held the gate open and waited impatiently for the others to go through. Which in the end they did; Frizz decidedly nervous, Lily a bit wary, and Keri bold as always. I don't think Keri would ever be afraid of anything. She would probably walk through the middle of a herd of Highland cattle.

I could see Mum's car, over on the far side. Bundle could obviously see it, too; or maybe he could smell it. We set off at a run. Keri cried, "Yee ha!" and came galloping after, with Lily prancing at her side and Frizz flolloping along behind in her squidgy sandals.

Well! You can maybe guess what happened… She went and stepped in a cowpat. Splat! Right in the middle of it. She gave this loud squawk and we all turned to look, thinking a cow had suddenly gone for her. (Not that a cow would. They're ever such peaceable creatures.)

"What are you doing?" yelled Keri.

Frizz was standing on one foot, flapping the other in the air, with tears streaming down her cheeks. "I've trodden in muck!"

It had squelched up, all green and gooey, inside her sandal, between her toes. She wasn't even wearing socks!

"It's horrible," wailed Frizz. "It's all cold and clammy!"

"It's only a cowpat," I said.

"But it *smells!*"

Actually, as a matter of fact, I think cowpats smell quite pleasant. All full of hay and grass. But I suppose it might not be so nice squashing up between your toes.

We urged her to just keep on walking and try to forget about it.

"It'll soon dry," said Keri.

"Yes, and we're nearly back," I said, "then you can rush home and jump in a bath."

Trust Frizz, I thought, for the second time. It would be her that had to go and tread in a cowpat. She stood there weeping, with one foot held up in the air, saying that it smelt. Lily and I took out our hankies and offered them, but she just daubed at herself in a helpless fashion and went on weeping.

In the end it was Keri who came to the rescue. "Oh, look here!" she said. "Take my socks!" And she put a hand on Lily's shoulder to steady herself, yanked off her wellies, removed her socks and thrust them at a blubbing Frizz. "Put these on, then you won't feel it."

"But w-what about y-you?" hiccupped Frizz, smearing the back of her hand across her face.

"Don't worry about me," said Keri. "I'll be all right."

"But your b-boots will r-rub if you don't have any s-socks!"

"So they'll rub," said Keri. "Who cares? What's the point of being friends if we can't give our socks to each other when we need them?"

I got all guilty afterwards and thought that I was supposed to be Frizz's best friend. I should have been the one to offer her my socks! I was too busy being mad at her and thinking what a wet blanket she was. Making all that fuss about a harmless little cowpat! How geeky could you get?

The following Saturday it was Lily's turn to choose and

we all went into town to join one of the dance sessions.

"I picked the three o'clock one," said Lily, "'cos it's disco dancing. I thought you'd like that."

Frizz whispered, "I'm no good at disco dancing!"

I whispered back, "Neither am I! But it doesn't matter, nobody'll notice."

I did my best to worm my way into the middle, 'cos then I reckoned with so many kids taking part I wouldn't be seen. There were all these people gazing down at us from the first floor of the shopping centre, and it made me feel really self-conscious! I didn't know where Frizz had got to. We were together for a bit, just at first, but then we got separated, and I was, like, hemmed in. I saw Keri, energetically throwing herself about, and Lily way down at the front, but I couldn't see Frizz anywhere.

I still couldn't see her even when the session came to an end.

"*Now* where has she gone?" said Keri.

We finally discovered her sitting on a seat outside Woolworth's.

"What happened?" cried Lily. "Why did you leave?"

You'll never believe what she said... She said that a boy had laughed at her!

"I'd have laid one on him if he'd dared to laugh at me!" said Keri.

Frizz had just turned tail and gone running off to hide.

"You really must learn to have a bit more *backbone*," said Keri. "Stick up for yourself! No one else is going to."

So that was the dancing. Next Saturday was Keri's choice, when we all went ice skating. Keri goes ice skating all the time and is a whizz. She just zooms and zips and flashes about all over. This is because she has been having lessons since she was about nine years old.

Lily has never had lessons but thanks to her dance training she has this incredible sense of balance. Lily could probably walk across a high wire without falling off. I couldn't! I would only have to look down just once and that would be it. A-a-a-a-rrrrgh! I would be hurtling head-first into space. I have no sense of balance at all! Keri said that every time she turned round she found me sitting on my bottom on the ice. "Polly, you are not meant to skate on your bum!" she said.

Frizz thought this was very funny. She laughed so

much that she ended up on *her* bum, next to me.

"Oh, get up, the pair of you!" cried Keri.

I got up, but Frizz didn't.

"What's the matter?" I said.

In a small voice Frizz said, "I've hurt my ankle."

"Oh, for heaven's sake!" Keri rolled her eyes. I knew what she was thinking: trust Frizz!

Frizz probably knew it, too.

We helped her up and she hobbled to the side. Lily came gliding over, wanting to know what was wrong.

"She's done her ankle in," said Keri; and she rolled her eyes again, at Lily this time.

"I'm sorry," whispered Frizz.

To be honest, I was half expecting her to burst into tears, I mean twisting your ankle is a lot worse, I would have thought, than just stepping in a cowpat, but she was obviously determined to be brave. Lily asked her if she thought she ought to go to hospital (Keri rolled her eyes for the third time) but Frizz shook her head and said she would be all right. "I'll just sit down here and wait. You go on skating."

"Are you sure?" I said.

"Yes." Frizz nodded, emphatically. 'It's already not hurting quite so much."

So we went back on to the ice and did our best to

just carry on and enjoy ourselves. Lily said, "Poor old Frizz", but Keri said scornfully that Frizz could be such a baby at times. "All that fuss about just twisting her ankle! I twisted mine once, playing hockey. I didn't go and sit down! I just carried on."

"It did look quite painful," I said, trying to be loyal to Frizz.

"Yes, but it's not like she's broken it, or anything."

She might not have broken it, but when Keri's mum came to collect us Frizz had to hop on one leg to the car and her ankle was really swollen, so that I thought Keri was being a bit unfair to say about her making a fuss. All the same, it did seem as if we couldn't ever go anywhere or do anything without Frizz having some kind of problem.

I said this to Mum when I got home. She wanted to know if I'd had a nice time and I said, "Yes, but Frizz went and ruined things again. She ruins everything!" And I told her how she had trodden in the cowpat when we went for our walk, and how she had run away to hide in the shopping centre all because a boy had laughed at her. "And now she's gone and fallen down and hurt her ankle!"

Mum said, "Oh, dear! Poor Dawn. She is in the wars, isn't she?"

"I just don't see why it has to keep happening," I said. "Why always *her*?"

"She's accident-prone," said Mum. "Probably because she hasn't got much confidence. She's very unsure of herself. It's all right for you and the others, you've all got your own things. But what has Dawn got?"

"I don't know," I said. "But I'm getting sick of it!"

Chapter 7

That night in bed I lay awake and thought about Frizz. And as usual, when I thought about her, these huge feelings of guilt washed over me. How could I have been so mean to her? How could I say that I was sick of her? She couldn't help being accident-prone. She couldn't help it if she wasn't more confident. It probably just meant that she wasn't as conceited as the rest of us. Like we all had these really high opinions of ourselves, what with Keri being so cool and Lily being so gifted and me being so *clever*. You never heard Frizz boasting, or puffing herself up. And

I knew her mum and dad didn't have much money and that sometimes Frizz had to wear clothes that came from places like Oxfam, so how could I have been so horrid, going on at her about her wellies and her shoes? *Embarrassing* her. I hated myself for doing that!

And then I thought how she hadn't told me her big secret, and I thought, "Yes, and that was really mean of her!" Trying to make myself feel a bit better. A bit less guilty. Like, she was mean to me before I was mean to her, sort of thing.

Why *hadn't* she told me? She'd never properly explained. Just muttered about "people talking all the time". For a minute I got a bit frothed up about it, a bit self-righteous, thinking to myself that "I would have told *her*!"

And then it occurred to me…what she'd meant by saying that people talked all the time. Maybe we'd all been so busy going on about ourselves, Keri and Lily and me, that Frizz had simply never had a chance. We'd heard all about Lily being a dragonfly and about Madame Assante asking her to show off her dancing to the rest of the class. We'd heard all about Keri being chosen for her hockey team (and all her other teams) and scoring lots of goals and being called on to the platform at morning assembly. We'd heard all about me being on the editorial committee and writing my poem and learning Latin. I had *boasted* about my Latin. I had been a right big head. And Frizz had just sat there and listened as we all splurged on about how brilliant we were. And we'd never really stopped to wonder what she was up to, or what was going on in her life!

Even when Keri had asked her if she was still doing her cooking, she hadn't asked because she *cared*. She'd asked because she'd felt it was her duty. Like when grown-ups suddenly decide they ought to take notice of you, and they put on big soapy beams and start asking these really sad questions like how old are you, and where do you go to school, and what are you going to do when you grow up. And you just know they're not really interested!

Keri hadn't really been interested. None of us had. After all, it was only Frizz. What could she have to say? It would have been different if she'd pushed herself forward and told us how her cookery teacher had said she'd baked the best cake in the class, or that hers was the only one that hadn't sunk in the middle (or whatever it is that cakes do). But Frizz isn't like that. She's too modest. And cooking just doesn't seem as exciting, somehow, as being in Madame Assante's class or scoring goals in hockey matches or having poems published in the school magazine.

"I scored three goals!"

Hey! Wow! Big round of applause.

"I baked a cake!"

So what?

It didn't seem fair; but as Craig keeps pointing out to me, whenever I am in a self-pitying mood, "Life isn't!"

That still wasn't any excuse for being mean to Frizz. So I sat up in bed and switched on my bedside lamp and for the first time in ages made an entry in my diary:

New resolution: from now on I am going to be nicer to Frizz!

I rang her the next morning to ask how her ankle was.

"It's all puffed up," she said.

"Oh." I'd been hoping she'd say it was all right. "Does it still hurt?"

Frizz said, "Yes, it's really painful. I can't walk on it. Mum's put a bandage on. I don't think I'll be able to go to school tomorrow."

"Oh! Poor you!" I didn't know what else to say. "Anyway," I said, "it means next Saturday we'd better just meet at your place, same as usual."

"I can't make it next Saturday," said Frizz.

"What? Why not?" I was used to Lily or Keri sometimes not being able to turn up, but not Frizz! Frizz was always there.

"I'm doing something," she said.

"What?"

"Just something."

She wouldn't tell me, no matter how I prodded. I thought, *more* secrets! And just for a moment I got all hot and cross. She was at it again! Keeping things from me. And then I remembered my resolution that I had written in my diary, and I swallowed and breathed very deeply and counted up to ten, and guess what? It worked!

Frizz wanted to know if I was mad at her, and I assured her that I wasn't. Which was true. I was keeping to my resolution!

"I *will* tell you," said Frizz. "I promise!"

"So long as you do," I said.

"I will," she said. "Honest!"

I said, "You'd better!" but not, like, threatening. More like...jokey. 'Cos I'd been cross with her too often. And she was still my best friend even if she was keeping secrets. All the same, I wished I knew what was going on!

We met at Keri's the following Saturday; just the three of us. It seemed very strange. There had been three of us before when someone couldn't make it. But we had never been three without Frizz!

We started off with our usual splash-about in the pool. Keri dived, Lily dog-paddled, I did my boring breaststroke. For once I didn't have to worry about Frizz, all by herself in the shallow end. Then Lily suddenly said, "Isn't it odd? I keep looking for her!"

"Me, too," I said.

"I keep thinking she's here!"

"We ought to teach her how to swim," said Keri. "She'd have more fun if she could swim!"

We left the pool and went up to Keri's room, where we did our best to carry on the same way we always did.

Lily told us her latest Madame Assante story. "This girl came to class wearing *fishnet tights.*"

Gasp, horror!

"Madame refused to teach her. She screamed, 'You! Out! Out, out, out! Tights with holes I will not have!'"

Keri told us how she and Mima were learning to

ride side-saddle so they could be eighteenth-century ladies in a pageant that was going to be held in the school grounds. "Mima fell off, but I didn't! I took to it straight away. It's actually quite easy. Well, it is for me!"

I started to recite another poem that I'd done – and then stopped after the first line. It suddenly seemed too much like showing off. And quite honestly, none of it was working anyway. Not Lily's story, not Keri's story, not my poem.

"It just seems all wrong," said Lily, "without Frizz!"

Even Keri agreed that she missed her.

Lily crinkled her nose. "Why's she gone all secretive on us, all of a sudden?"

I was about to say that I thought perhaps it might be our fault – all yammering and yacking and mouthing off, and never giving her a chance – when surprise, surprise! Keri said it for me. "You don't think it's us, do you?"

"Us?" said Lily. "What d'you mean?"

"Well!" Keri waved a hand. "The way we've treated her...making her feel she's nothing but a nuisance."

"Mm." Lily thought about it. "I suppose we have been a bit horrid to her."

"Some of us have been really mean," said Keri. I

thought at first she meant me, but Keri is one of those people, she can really surprise you. She didn't mean me, she meant her! "I felt like *screaming*," she said, "when she did her ankle in!"

I said, "I felt like screaming when she turned up for our walk wearing sandals. *And* when she trod in the cowpat! At least you gave her your socks to wear."

"Well, I felt sorry for her," said Keri. "She looked so pathetic, standing there...all covered in cowpat."

"And then there was that boy, laughing at her," said Lily.

"And I told her she ought to learn to stick up for herself! Which she should. She lets herself be pushed around far too much. Mainly by me," confessed Keri. "I know I'm a bit bossy, but you two stand up to me! You don't let me walk all over you."

"Frizz is too meek," I said. And I told them how I'd stayed awake the whole night through thinking about Frizz and the way we'd behaved towards her. All about us going on about ourselves and the things we'd done, and poor old Frizz never being given a chance.

"Why is she so *modest*?" burst out Lily. "Why does she let us do it?"

"'Cos that's Frizz," I said.

"But we all sit and boast and she never says a thing!"

"Maybe" – Keri said it slowly – "maybe she hasn't got anything to say. I'm not being nasty! But we're all achieving like crazy; I mean Lily's got her dancing and you've got your writing—"

"And you're in all the teams...but what has Frizz got?"

I said that was the point Mum had made. "She says that we've all got something, but Frizz hasn't got anything, and that's why she lacks confidence and treads in cowpats and busts up her ankle."

"Oh!" cried Lily. "You've made me feel dreadful. I wish there was something we could do!"

"Yes. Something...you know! To make her feel better," said Keri.

"It would be even nicer," I said, "if there was something *Frizz* could do. It's so horrid if we're all achieving and she isn't!"

"What is she good at? Think of something she's good at!"

We all sat and thought.

"She's good at cooking," I said.

"Mm..." Keri seemed dubious. "Isn't there anything else?"

"Why, what's wrong with cooking?" said Lily.

Keri said there wasn't anything wrong with it. "But you can't get into a *cooking* team or be on a *cooking* committee or go to *cooking* school."

"You might be able to," I said.

"It's not the same! Think of something else."

So we all sat there, thinking as hard as we could, when there was a sudden cry of "Keri! Turn the television on!" and Keri's mum burst into the room without even bothering to knock. "Quick!" she said. "Quick! Turn it on!"

Keri has her own TV, natch. Just as well, or we would have missed it. Frizz's secret! The big event! We were just in time to hear a voice announcing, "The winner of the Schools Junior Chef of the Year Competition... Dawn Frizzell, of Heathfield High!"

And there she was! Our Frizz! All blushing and bashful on the television!

We all screeched. Lily jumped up and punched the air. I wailed, "Why didn't she tell us?"

But I was too excited to be cross! My friend Frizz...on the television! I could hardly believe it.

"Way to go!" cried Keri.

Keri's mum said, "Imagine that! Little Dawn...she's always so quiet. Now all of a sudden she's a celebrity!"

Our Frizz…a celeb!

It was humbling to think that all the time we'd been sitting there feeling superior, feeling sorry for her, racking our brains what we could do to make her feel better, Frizz had been out there, doing her own thing and never saying a word. And here she was, Junior Chef of the Year! Which, as Keri said, put all our puny little achievements well in the shade.

"We ought to send her a card!" cried Lily. "A *well done* card!" But sending a card seemed a bit tame. We wanted to do something now. Immediately!

"If only she had a moby," said Keri. "Then we could text her."

"Or send an email," I said, "if she had a computer."

It was Keri's mum who came up with the best idea.

"Her mum and dad run a shop, they're bound to have an answer phone. You could always ring up and ask if you can leave a message. Then it would be there waiting for her when she got home."

So that was what we did! First off, Frizz's dad answered the phone, and I told him what we wanted to do.

"That would be ace," he said. "She'd like that. I'll

tell her the minute she gets in. Off you go, then! Leave your message."

So we dialled again, and this time it went on to the answering machine. Lily, because she is the only one of us who can sing in tune, sang *Congratulations*, then we all put our heads together and shouted "WELL DONE!" just as loudly as we possibly could.

Keri's mum said, "Well! I should think she ought to be able to hear that!"

Suddenly, overnight, our friend Frizz had become famous! She was interviewed on the radio, both locally and nationally. And she had her picture in all the local papers. The big one and the freebies.

We met at her place the following Saturday. Keri wanted to know if it was all right for us to come in. "Or are you too grand to talk to us?"

Frizz giggled and said, "I'll never be too grand! Not even when I'm top chef at the Savoy!"

"Oh," said Keri. "So that's what you're going to be?"

"Well, or the Ritz," said Frizz. "Though actually, probably, I'll have my own restaurant. And you can all come and eat there!"

"For free?" said Lily.

"Reduced rates," said Frizz.

We went up to her room and she told us all about the competition and what she had cooked and what it was like being on television. "We had to plan this three-course meal and I said I wanted to do cordon vert and my teacher said she didn't think that was a good idea 'cos they'd all expect a meat dish, but I wanted to 'cos I really enjoy doing veggie stuff. When I have my restaurant it's going to be a veggie one. But haute cuisine, you know?"

We nodded, solemnly. Oat cuisine. Absolutely!

"Sounds lovely," said Lily.

"Yes. Well, I decided I was going to start with something simple. Avocado mousse," said Frizz. "Then I thought I'd do a nut roast, with *white* nuts, and serve it with new potatoes and beans. Then I'd finish with strawberry and cashew nut ice cream, 'cos that is really scrummy and I've got some in the fridge that we can eat for tea. But I never ever thought I'd win," said Frizz. "I mean, I just never thought I'd stand a chance! Most of the others were, like, thirteen or fourteen, you know? And nobody else was doing cordon vert. But it was just this feeling I had, that it was what I wanted to do. The best chefs only ever do things they want to do. Like roast beef and two veg, *no way*!"

We shook our heads.

"No way!" said Keri.

"But it was really scary, in front of the cameras." Frizz made her eyes go big. "You just have to pretend they're not there or you'd get so nervous you'd start spilling everything and dropping everything. Like one boy, he was doing this flambé dish and it all went up in flames! WHOOSH! I mean, a flambé is meant to go up in flames, but it's not meant to go *whoosh*!" Frizz giggled. "Anyway," she said, "what about you guys? What have you been up to?"

There was a silence.

"Oh! This and that," said Keri.

"Have you scored any more goals?"

"Mm…one or two."

"What about Lily? Are you still Madame Assante's favourite?"

"Well, she hasn't thrown her stick at me yet," said Lily.

"Oh, she won't!" said Frizz. "She likes you." She turned to me. "Pollee! Have you written any more poems?"

"I did do one," I said.

"Aren't you going to read it?"

I was quite tempted. I mean, it was a good poem.

One of my best! But this was Frizz's day. I could read my poem another time. I'd rather hear more about you," I said.

"Yes!" Lily settled herself into a more comfortable listening position. "Tell us what it was like when you were waiting to hear who'd won!"

"Did you get a funny feeling in the pit of your stomach?" said Keri.

"Well..." Frizz took a breath. "Actually, if you want to know, I thought I was going to throw up! They said who'd come third, and they said who'd come second—"

And then they'd said who'd come first, and it was Frizz. Our friend Frizz. And we were all DEAD PROUD.

About the Author

Jean Ure had her first book published while she was still at school and immediately went rushing out into the world declaring that she was AN AUTHOR. But it was another few years before she had her second book published, and during that time she had to work at lots of different jobs to earn money. In the end she went to drama school to train as an actress. While she was there she met her husband and wrote another book. She has now written more than eighty books! She lives in Croydon with her husband and their family of seven rescued dogs and four rescued cats.

Girlfriends

Find out whether the Gang of Four stay friends for
ever in the next book in the series!

978 1 84616 964 9 £4.99

Chapter 1

"So, you guys!" Keri hoisted herself up onto my window ledge. "What gives?"

Lily and I looked at each other. I giggled; Lily pulled a face. Keri was at it again...trying to be oh, so cool!

She is quite cool, actually; but sometimes she just, like, overdoes it. And Frizz didn't understand her, anyway. In tones of puzzlement, she said, "*What gives?*"

"That's right, kiddo!" Keri punched the air. "What gives! Meaning," she added kindly, in normal everyday English, "what's new in your life?"

Keri was obviously in a good mood. Ordinarily she would have got impatient, but today she was sounding well pleased with herself.

It was Saturday afternoon, and for once we had all turned up. Lily, Keri, Frizz and me. The Gang of Four! (Plus Bundle, who is my dog.) It was our last meeting before the summer holidays, so we'd all made an extra-special effort. Just recently, we'd had rather a lot of meetings where there'd only been three of us, or sometimes even just two. Once or twice we'd even had to cancel. It wasn't that we were losing interest, or stopping being friends, or anything like that; just that the summer term had been so-o-o busy.

For all of us! Even for Frizz, who had simply hated her first term at Heathfield. But she'd settled down, now, and made some friends, and even joined the drama club. I could hardly believe it! Frizz, joining the drama club! Frizz. Who used to be so shy she wouldn't even put up her hand in class to answer a question! She was really coming out of her shell.

It was since she'd won the Junior Schools Chef of the Year Competition and been on the telly and had her picture in all the local newspapers. It hadn't made her big-headed, because Frizz isn't like that, but it did seem to have given her lashings of confidence. Which was nice as it meant the rest of us didn't have to feel guilty when good things happened to us, such as, for example, me getting a poem in the school magazine, or Keri scoring goals in a hockey match, or Lily being chosen for special dance classes. That sort of thing. We didn't have to feel responsible. Before it had always been, "What about Frizz? Poor old Frizz!" She wasn't poor old Frizz any more and it was a great weight off our minds.

Plus, of course, we were genuinely happy for her. And proud! I'd told everyone at school, "That was my friend Frizz on the telly." I couldn't help doing a little bit of boasting. I was friends with a celeb!

Lily is another celeb, or is going to be. She is going to be a famous dancer and people the world over will drink champagne from her ballet shoes. (Pink satin, natch!) Frizz is going to be a famous chef and have her own restaurant (*cordon vert*, which means veggie) and Keri is just going to be Keri (and will probably be famous just for that). I don't yet know what I am going to be. Whatever it is, I don't expect I shall be famous. Boo hoo! But I don't really mind. When you are little and round – well, roundish – you are probably not cut out for fame. And anyway, what a drag! People wanting your autograph all the time, and recognising you wherever you go. I especially wouldn't want to be recognised when I am taking Bundle round the park, as I am usually to be seen in a disgusting old anorak and muddy wellies. "Yeeurgh! Look!" (People would go.) "That's Polly Roberts... What a sight!"

So I think I'll just stay anonymous, and let the rest of them twinkle and shine. It doesn't bother me one little bit!

I beamed round at them as they sat there in my

bedroom – Keri perched on the window ledge, with her feet propped on a chair, Lily cross-legged on the floor and Frizz flopped on the bed, with Bundle stretched out beside her. These were my friends! My very best friends, that I'd known since way back. Year Two, Year Three. We'd all been at different schools since September. Lily was at her dancing school, Frizz was at Heathfield, Keri (whose mum and dad are seriously rich) at her posh boarding school and me at the High School, which Frizz calls the Boffin School.

My mum and dad are not seriously rich, since money does not, as Mum is forever telling me, grow on trees, so I'd had to get a scholarship, which was what made Frizz call me Boffin Head, which I used to wish she wouldn't. She doesn't do it so much any more; she stopped after she became a celeb. It was like, now we were equals. I was a boffin head; she was a celeb!

We'd all made this vow, before we left Juniors, that we'd still go on being the Gang of Four. We were going to meet up every Saturday, taking it in turns whose place we'd go to. And we had! All through the winter term, all through the spring term, all through the summer. But now it was holidays, which meant this might be our last meeting for a while. Which was why we'd all made an effort and turned up.

"So, you guys!" That was Keri, leaning forward on her window ledge (and nearly overbalancing). "What's new?" Keri hadn't been at the last meeting; she'd gone off to do things with her friend Jemima. "What's been happening?"

"We've broken up," said Frizz. "Two months of freedom, yum yum yum!"

"Utter bliss," agreed Keri.

"I've got stuff to do," I said. "Simply masses of it!"

"Stuff?" said Keri. "What sort of stuff?"

"Essays and stuff. Summer homework."

Frizz pulled a face and said, "Boffin school!"

I told her that I didn't really mind. "I quite like working."

Frizz and Keri looked at each other and shook their heads. Which was something they'd never have done before Frizz became a celeb.

"Well, whatever turns you on," drawled Keri.

Lily piped up from the floor (where she was busy contorting herself into odd shapes). "I still have to practise every day."

"Oh. Well! You," said Keri. "You're a dancer. That's different."

I didn't quite see why. Lily has to exercise her body, I have to exercise my mind; Lily likes stretching and bending, I like reading and writing. Why should Keri sneer at me and not at Lily? 'Cos I knew that was what she was doing. Oh, Polly. She's just a boffin. It really annoys me! But I didn't say anything 'cos of it being our last meeting until (probably) next term. I didn't want to make waves or anything.

"So where's everybody going?" said Keri. "What's everybody's plans?" She was just dying to tell us hers!

Read the rest of

Boys Are
OK!

to find out what happens next…

£4.99   978 1 84616 961 8

Pink knickers aren't cool!

Neither is Jessamy James, their owner. Nor is going to secondary school...especially if the gang of four have to split up! But bad boys and bad underwear are nothing compared with the problems facing Polly and the girlfriends' future.

Can they stick together, or will they end up being torn apart?

978 1 84616 963 2

£4.99

Despite being at her new school with
the uncool Jessamy James, Polly's making plenty
of new friends and earning herself a whole new
social life. But will new arrangements clash with
the gang of four's weekly Saturday meet-ups?

Will Polly be facing a friendship crisis? Or will the
girlfriends work it out?

Girlfriends

More Orchard Red Apples

❑ Pink Knickers Aren't Cool!	*Jean Ure*	978 1 84616 961 8
❑ Girls Stick Together!	*Jean Ure*	978 1 84616 963 2
❑ Girls Are Groovy!	*Jean Ure*	978 1 84616 962 5
❑ Boys Are OK!	*Jean Ure*	978 1 84616 964 9
❑ Do Not Read This Book	*Pat Moon*	978 1 84121 435 1
❑ Do Not Read Any Further	*Pat Moon*	978 1 84121 456 6
❑ Do Not Read Or Else!	*Pat Moon*	978 1 84616 082 0
❑ The Shooting Star	*Rose Impey*	978 1 84362 560 5
❑ My Scary Fairy Godmother	*Rose Impey*	978 1 84362 683 1
❑ Hothouse Flower	*Rose Impey*	978 1 84616 215 2
❑ Introducing Scarlett Lee	*Rose Impey*	978 1 84616 706 5 *
❑ The Truth About Josie Green	*Belinda Hollyer*	978 1 84362 885 9
❑ Secrets, Lies & My Sister Kate	*Belinda Hollyer*	978 1 84616 690 7 *

All priced at £4.99, apart from those marked * which are £5.99.
Orchard Red Apples are available from all good bookshops,
or can be ordered direct from the publisher:
Orchard Books, PO BOX 29, Douglas IM99 1BQ
Credit card orders please telephone 01624 836000
or fax 01624 837033
or e-mail: bookshop@enterprise.net for details.

To order please quote title, author and ISBN
and your full name and address.
Cheques and postal orders should be made payable to 'Bookpost plc.'
Postage and packing is FREE within the UK
(overseas customers should add £1.00 per book).

Prices and availability are subject to change.